CROSSING THE LINE

NICOLA MARSH

Copyright © Nicola Marsh 2014
Published by Nicola Marsh 2014

All the characters in this book have no existence outside the imagination of the author and have no relation whatsoever to anyone bearing the same name or names. They're not distantly inspired by any individual known or unknown to the author and all the incidents in the book are pure invention.

All rights reserved including the right of reproduction in any form. The text or any part of the publication may not be reproduced or transmitted in any form without the written permission of the publisher.

The author acknowledges the copyrighted or trademarked status and trademark owners of the word marks mentioned in this work of fiction.

Laying it all on the line for love…

I'm tired of being good.

Achieving geek status at college doesn't equate with fun. So when I head home to my dad's tennis academy in Santa Monica on spring break, I'm determined to be bad. And hot Aussie tennis star Kye Sheldon is the perfect guy to help me break all the rules.

However, Kye's troubled past continues to dog him and attending the Cresswell Tennis Academy is his last chance at the big time. He can't afford to screw up…by screwing me, the boss's daughter.

But our relationship is much more than a vacation fling. Will it be game, set, match, when the truth is revealed?

Or will we have a real shot at love-all?

AUTHOR'S NOTE

In this story, Kye Sheldon is Australian.

Here's clarification of the 'Aussie-isms' Kye uses:

Pansy-arsed – lame
arse – ass
coldie – beer
soft drink – soda
piss-poor – weak
holiday – vacation
windscreen – windshield
trannies – transvestites
mobile – cell phone
soft-cock – pathetic
fortnight – two weeks
belly-up – wrecked
dropkicked – hurt
fairy floss – cotton candy
pansy – feminine

ONE
MIA

"You should do him." My BFF Dani pointed to a six-four dork in a custom-made suit sucking up to my dad next to the trophy cabinet. "Big hands. Big feet."

I rolled my eyes. "You don't actually believe that crap, do you?"

Dani sniggered. "Considering the amount of first hand research I've done, I think I'm a fairly good judge."

I hated how Dani did that, perpetuating the slut label she'd copped at high school. Dani liked to date. A lot. That didn't equate to sleeping around. But the fact she was blonde, gorgeous and had a great rack meant jealous girls had been happy to spread rumors. What made me madder? Rather than defend herself, she played up to it.

"Why do you still do that when we left high school three years ago?"

She ignored my question and tapped my nose. "Almost forgot. Big nose equals big dick too."

As usual, I didn't push her on an issue she knew bugged the hell out of me. I swatted away her finger. "He's not my type."

"Is anyone your type?" She grabbed two champagne flutes from a passing waiter and handed me one. "You've been here an hour and I haven't seen you scope out a single guy."

No great surprise. I returned home to my dad's place, the legendary Cresswell Tennis Academy in Santa Monica, every spring break, and not once had I found a guy remotely 'scope-worthy'. Egotistical sport junkies weren't my thing.

"That's because I'm so damn happy to see you again." I slid my arm around her waist and hugged tight. "I've missed you, sweetie."

"You're such a sap," she said, returning my semi-hug before easing away to down her champagne. "Let's get drunk and pick up the cutest guys here for a night of raunchy fun."

Another thing that pissed me off about Dani. We hadn't seen each other since last spring break, and our first night together she'd rather hook up with some anonymous guy than hang out with me.

I would've preferred to stay in tonight, watching corny old DVDs and eating ice cream from the tub while we caught up on gossip. Instead, Dani had arrived at my villa an hour ago, demanding I attend this lame party my dad was throwing for the new academy peeps.

I hated my dad's parties at the academy. Wall to wall tennis jocks whose egos matched their oversized racket collection, my dad's boring friends, and the general hangers-on who thought my dad walked on water because he'd won a record number of Grand Slams. Minimal food, maximum alcohol and requisite fake schmoozing. Country club exclusivity with an overload of testosterone.

But I couldn't say no to Dani. She was the only thing I

missed about Santa Monica—discounting Dad—and we could hang out at some boring party for a while before doing our catch up over a Cookies'n'Cream tub later.

"That's an oxymoron. Cute guys here and raunchy fun." I glanced around, not seeing a single guy I'd give my phone number to let alone allow to touch me.

Dani's wide-eyed fake innocence didn't fool me for a second. "You sure you're not still a virgin?"

I snorted. "You know I lost my virginity to Andy in high school."

I hadn't told her about the only other time I'd had sex, with one of my friends at DU. And that had only been in the last few months. Pitiful, considering I'd been at the University of Denver for the last few years.

"That pencil dick? Time to find yourself a real man."

I stifled a giggle at Dani's accurate assessment of Andy's appendage. "How did you know he was a pencil dick?"

Dani rolled her eyes. "Babe, I could tell you the size, girth and prowess of every dickwad's cock at Dumbass High."

And there she went again, pissing me off. I knew for a fact she didn't sleep around that much back then. Now? I wouldn't know. Sure, Dani was her usual joking self when we Skyped weekly and emailed a few times a month, but the truth was I had no idea what my best friend did with her spare time these days. And by her account, there was a lot of that.

Dani lived off her trust fund. She didn't work. She didn't do charity. And she didn't let me into her life anymore. Not like she used to.

Everything changed when she backed out of college before we were due to start. She never told me why. Gave some lame-ass excuse about not being interested in going it alone when she had her family's money to live off. Which I didn't believe for a second, considering Dani was the most independent person I knew and couldn't wait to join me at DU.

But I hadn't pushed because my BFF had looked seriously fragile at the time, like a Santa Ana wind could blow her over with the faintest gust. The flu, she'd said. I'd been terrified it had been something more serious. So I gave her the space she'd requested to get her shit together and when she finally Skyped me three months later, the old Dani was back. Irreverent. Brash. Irrepressible.

I elbowed her. "If you slept with half the guys you say you have, you wouldn't be able to walk."

"Practice makes perfect." She winked and did a fair imitation of a wide-stance cowboy swagger.

I laughed and shook my head. "I've missed you."

"Same here, babe." She slung an arm around my shoulder. "But here's the deal. If you don't bag the hottest guy here tonight, I'm going to sign you up with every online dating site in Cali. And I'll use that pic of you with the mud mask that looked like you had shit smeared all over your face."

"Is that the best you can do?" My snooty glare failed when I chuckled.

She tapped her bottom lip, pretending to think. "If that doesn't do the trick, maybe I'll get my mom to tell your dad you're lonely and would appreciate a fix-up with one of his tennis protégés—"

"You wouldn't dare." Dani's mom was a shameless Hollywood socialite who made meddling in people's lives an art form. As for my dad, I'd already been subjected to his less than subtle matchmaking as a teenager, which is why

Dani's threat held serious fear factor. If those two got together on my behalf? A nunnery would be the only place I could escape their machinations.

Dani's grin was positively evil. "Try me."

I crossed my arms and puffed out a huffy breath. "Fine. I'm going to find the guy least like a tennis jock and do him tonight."

Translated: I'd walk up to him, beg him to play along with me long enough to get my trouble-making BFF off my case, then escape to my villa on the pretext I was spending the night with him.

I'd deal with telling Dani the truth in the morning.

"That's my girl." Dani tweaked my nose, grabbed my shoulders and twirled me in a slow three-sixty. "See anyone you fancy?"

Yeah, Ryan Gosling on the DVD cover of his latest movie, but that was back in my villa and unless I played along I'd be stuck here with Dani doing this all night.

Increasingly tired of Dani's never-ending need to hang out with a guy to make a party complete, I glanced around at the requisite tennis jocks in immaculate sports jackets, chinos and polo shirts. They chugged bottles of water, trying to make a good impression on my dad, the coaches and the rest of the academy crew. A few had potential in the looks department but they'd be too scared of pissing off my dad to play along with my lame scheme. No way would they leave with me with my dad looking on, on the pretense of screwing me or not.

And that's when I saw him.

The perfect guy.

Well, not *the* perfect guy, but the guy I knew could come through for me tonight.

He stood in the far corner of the room, away from the

crowd, partially hidden behind the pot-planted palms, strategically placed to offer some privacy for recalcitrant loners like him.

He wore a scowl along with dark denim, a blue sports jacket and a tight white T that even at this distance outlined a muscular chest. Brown hair. Chiseled jaw. Sexy mouth. Eye-catchingly gorgeous, if he ever stopped glowering.

"You found him?" Dani said, when she noticed I resisted further twirling.

"Yeah." I jerked my head toward the corner. "Him."

"Fuck," Dani murmured, staring at me with newfound admiration. "I like the way you think, babe. He's got sex god written all over him."

"And soon I'll be all over him," I said, injecting enough fake bravado to sound believable while thinking 'I wish'.

Because a small part of me did wish I had the guts to go after a guy like that. A guy who looked bad enough to help me break free of being good.

Maybe I should amend my plan from getting him to pretend to hang out with me to flirting relentlessly so we hung out for real?

How long since I'd had fun with a guy beyond study dates and coffee in the college cafeteria? My grades were good. My life was good. I was *good*. For once, I'd love to be bad.

"Go." Dani shoved me in the guy's direction. "Report back in the morning."

I wiggled my fingers in a saucy wave at Dani as I strode toward the guy, who'd just downed a soda in record time.

By the time I was half way across the crowded room, I saw him duck out onto the terrace, which wouldn't be opened until later in the evening.

So I did the only thing I could.

Took a short cut to the terrace and crossed my fingers I could pull this off.

TWO
KYE

The second I stepped into the function room at the Cresswell Tennis Academy, I couldn't breathe. A stifling combination of designer perfume, overcooked shrimp and jock testosterone hung in the air like a miasmic cloud. The kind of scene I despised.

I wanted to leave. Ditch this pansy-arse party and the pretentious stuffy tennis establishment, leave Santa Monica and head back to Sydney.

But I couldn't. That's the thing about final chances. Screw this up and I was in deep shit.

"Would you like a drink, Sir?"

Sir? Seriously? Even the staff in this joint acted like they had a pole stuck ten-feet up their arse.

I stared at the waiter, who looked roughly twenty-two like me, and automatically reached for a beer. A coldie would take the edge off.

A coldie would also make me crave another, then another, to help me forget every godforsaken reason I was stuck in this hellhole for the foreseeable future.

In the first wise decision I'd made in months, I chose a

soft drink instead. I downed it in three gulps and set the glass on a nearby table. I should mingle. I should do a lot of things according to my dad: lose the temper and the attitude, don't waste my talent and don't screw up.

Guess I should be grateful he hadn't disowned me after I'd busted that dweeb's nose back in Sydney. But even though we'd only known about each other for the last seven years, Dad stuck by me. He understood why I slugged the prick. No one got to call my mum a hooker, among other things, and get away with it.

"Drink, Sir—"

"No." I didn't want a frigging drink. I wanted to get the hell out of here. "Thanks," I said, softening my tone when the waitress stared at me with genuine fear.

Looked like I was failing with the change of attitude already. Not wasting my talent? Remained to be seen.

I could hit a ball around a court. Very well, according to the top coaches in Australia. The thing was, they didn't understand why I played tennis. Ironic, that the very attitude they wanted drummed out of me was what drove me to smash the shit out of that furry green ball.

When I saw another waiter bearing down on me with a sushi platter, I headed for the nearest exit. A locked French door leading out onto a semi-dark terrace. Seclusion. Perfect.

I flicked the lock and stepped out onto the slate tiled terrace that overlooked the pristine grass courts. Ten in total, with another ten clay and ten indoor surfaced behind the clubhouse. I couldn't fault the facilities here. The rest? Remained to be seen.

I propped against the wall and stared at the first court, the one I'd toured earlier with Dirk Cresswell, the academy's CEO. Dirk may be legendary in American tennis circles, with his record Grand Slam wins and golden boy charm, but from the fifteen minutes he'd taken to show me around today, he seemed like a self-absorbed, pompous prick. Who I had to play nice with if I didn't want to be turfed out on my arse.

"Hey."

I turned toward the girl's voice as she stepped out of the shadows, not sure what annoyed me most. The intrusion or the way she sauntered toward me, all long legs and cocky smile.

She was just my type: tall, sexy brunette with enough hip sway to make a guy wonder what made her so confident, and bedroom eyes that hinted at sin.

Sadly, this devil had just landed in the City of Angels and sin was the last thing on my agenda.

"I'm not in the mood for company," I said, expecting her to head back inside.

She didn't falter as she strode toward me. "Too bad, because I needed some air and this terrace is big enough for the both of us."

I could've left but there was something in the way she was staring at me that had me intrigued: like she wanted me but wouldn't have a clue what to do if she got me.

"Mia." She stuck out her hand. "Pleased to meet you."

"Kye." I reluctantly shook her hand. "Wish I could say the same."

"You don't like girls?" She slid her hand out of mine, the insolent quirk of her lips making me want to do something I shouldn't. Like kiss the smirk off her smart mouth.

"Love women." I took a step back, staring at her feet and slowly sweeping upward in a deliberate perusal meant to make a point. I wanted to make her squirm. It backfired, as I noted red nail polish matching her towering shoes, slim ankles, long legs, tight black dress that ended mid-thigh and hugged her lean bod, and pert tits. The frigging dress had a front zipper that just begged to be undone. Beyond hot.

By the time I reached her face, she was blushing.

"So which am I?" She leaned forward, giving me a generous glimpse of cleavage. "Girl or woman?"

If I were in the mood to flirt, Mia would've been perfect. I knew her type in a heartbeat. Good girl wanting to dabble. Her country club folks were probably inside sipping martinis and kissing arse. And Mia wanted to flirt with the jocks for a night, without the pressure of having to put out. I'd love to see how far I could push her, call her bluff. Instead, I had to drive her away before I did something stupid.

I'd had these moods before. I was better off alone.

"Honestly?"

She nodded, so I gave it to her straight.

"You're a college girl on spring break looking for a little down and dirty fun. Your folks probably drive a SUV, have dinner at the country club every night and play piss-poor tennis here weekly."

I saw hurt flicker in her big, brown eyes. Good. The faster she left, the better. So I drove the boot in harder.

"You want to slum it for a while, have a little holiday fun. String some poor dumb-arse tennis rookie along before giving him a severe case of blue-balls."

I deliberately turned my back on her. "Maybe the Aussie accent fooled you into thinking I'm that dumb-arse? But sorry, kid, you're definitely a girl and I only fool around with women."

I hated myself for treating someone I'd only just met like this. Mia whoever-she-was didn't deserve it, but the blackness was crowding in and I needed to escape.

Spying steps leading onto the lower level, I headed in that direction.

"My mom died when I was little. My dad drives a Mustang, drinks scotch and doesn't have to kiss anyone's ass."

I heard the hitch in her soft voice and it slayed me more than her admissions.

"Sure, I play *piss-poor* tennis, if that means I play badly. So I guess one out of four ain't bad." I heard the snap of her fingers. "Oh, and you were right about one thing. You're definitely a dumbass."

I should've kept walking. Headed straight for those steps without looking back. But the fact I'd misjudged her so badly stung real bad. Hadn't I busted that dickhead's nose in Sydney because he'd misjudged my mum? And me?

I'd put up with being misjudged my entire life: the poor kid from the Cross whose mum ran a strip joint. The kid who was probably a pimp. The kid who must do drugs because of where he lived.

I'd copped it all and hated every minute of it.

So why the hell had I just done the same to a woman I barely knew and who didn't deserve to bear the brunt of my foul mood?

I stopped and turned back to face her. "I'm sorry."

"Don't be." She waved away my apology. "You can't help being a dumbass. You were born that way."

I smiled. For the first time in a long time. "You're probably right."

"So what's with the mood?" She tilted her head to one side, studying me. "Because I know that wasn't all about me."

I shook my head. "You don't want to know."

"Maybe I do ..." She hesitated, uncertainty clouding her

eyes, before she straightened her shoulders. "You were right about one thing. I am in college. And I am on spring break." She puffed out a long breath. "This is my first night back home and I had to attend this stupid party, when it's the last thing I felt like doing, so I guess that makes us kindred spirits in a way."

"You don't know the first thing about me—"

"Chill." She rolled her eyes. "All I meant was you look like you don't want to be here. I definitely don't want to be here." She gestured at the tennis courts. "So why don't we ditch this lame-ass party and take a walk out there?"

She'd articulated my plan, with one flaw. I still wanted to be alone.

"I don't think so—"

"Shut up." She slipped her hand into mine before I could blink. "Let's go."

She tugged on my hand as I stared at our linked hands in disbelief. I had two options. Yank my hand free, make a big deal of this by stomping away and run the risk of her running to her daddy, who was probably besties with Dirk Cresswell. Or suck it up and leave like I'd intended. With a hanger-on.

"If we don't make a run for it now, the rest of the party will spill out here soon and then we'll be trapped."

I frowned, nodded. "Fine."

Though it wasn't, because as I allowed Mia to lead me down the steps, I wondered why I was still holding her hand. And enjoying it.

THREE
MIA

I was in way over my head with this one.

The guys I dated in college were ... sedate. Soft-spoken, laid-back guys who talked football and basketball and grades. Guys who were polite and refined. Guys who would play along with goofy crap like what I'd planned.

Guys the antithesis of Kye.

Oh. My. God. Dani had been right. Sex god.

Pity about the attitude.

I didn't go for surly bad boys. Rudeness annoyed me.

But I'd started down this track tonight and if there was one thing I always did, it was finish what I started.

Somehow, my plan had changed between the time I'd left Dani and the time I'd met Kye. Had to have been all of ten seconds from the time he'd stepped out onto the terrace and I'd introduced myself, but I'd known then he was more than a stooge to help me pull off a lame stunt.

There'd been something behind his glower ... a hint of vulnerability behind the sneer that made me wonder what a guy like him was doing here. He obviously didn't fit in and I knew the feeling.

As for his sexy Aussie accent? Yeah, that probably had something to do with the fact why I was still hanging around. If only I could encourage him to talk more.

"You can let go now," he said, his low tone making awareness ripple through me. "I won't make a break for it."

I squeezed his hand. "Why don't you let go?"

"Because I'm not the one holding on hard enough to crush every metatarsal in my hand."

"Someone's studying anatomy at college," I muttered, and didn't let go.

I liked holding Kye's hand. Liked the feel of his roughened palm, his strong fingers. Liked the false courage it gave me.

Because I feared if I let go, the last of my courage would disappear and I'd be the one bolting. Back to the safety of my villa, far away from badass Aussies with blue eyes and broad shoulders and a mouth I couldn't stop staring at.

Sadly, I could count the guys I'd made out with on one hand. Maybe two. But Kye's mouth? Made a good girl like me think very bad thoughts.

"I don't go to uni," he said. "But I fractured my hand once." He grimaced. "The pain of a fractured metatarsal is a bitch."

"How'd you do it?" I figured the longer I kept him talking and walking, the better my chances were of actually going through with this.

Because I had plans for Kye tonight. Big plans. Plans that were so far removed from my boring, mundane life that I needed to make this happen before I imploded.

"Punched a hole in a guy's windscreen."

I didn't like violence. I'd seen what it did to my roommate in freshman year, when her possessive ex wouldn't take no for an answer and ended up in prison after taking his frustrations out on her once too often.

While Kye had radiated hostility back there on the terrace, I didn't sense a violent undertone. Then, what did I know? I'd targeted him because he gave off a bad boy aura.

"Dare I ask why?"

His fingers flexed around mine. "Because he called my mum a whore." He paused. "And worse."

"That's harsh."

"I heard it a lot because of where we lived and what she did for a living."

Curiosity made me want to push him for answers, but I figured he'd told me more than he would have normally and silence would probably work better.

"We lived in Kings Cross, the seediest suburb in Sydney. In an apartment over a strip club. That Mum owned and ran." He spat the words almost defiantly, as if daring me to make a disparaging comment.

"If you're waiting for me to judge you, you'll be waiting a long time."

He sneered. "Good girls like you always judge guys like me."

And that's when I finally released his hand. Only because I planted both my hands on his chest and shoved.

"Want to know the truth? I did judge you tonight. When I saw you standing in that room, nursing a soda and a snarl, I said to myself 'that's the kind of guy I want to be with tonight because his shitty mood matches mine'. I wanted you to play along with a crazy plan I had to ditch the party, so I followed you onto the terrace. And I acted all brave and mouthy, when in fact you're the last type of guy I'd usually hang out with."

I shoved him again, working up a good head of steam.

"You're rude and condescending and obnoxious. And you're a judgmental dickwad." I dragged in a breath, surprised by the sting of indignant tears behind my eyelids. "So pardon me for just wanting to hang out with someone different tonight. Someone who's not from the cloying, smothering world I grew up in and moved several states away to escape."

Rant over, I let my arms fall to my sides. I shouldn't have shoved him. So much for my anti-violence stance. But a small part of me had to admit it felt good. Freaking great, in fact, to be assertive for once. Maybe the badass's bad attitude was catchy?

He stared at me, blue eyes narrowed, not moving a muscle. All that barely restrained tension should've intimidated me. It didn't. Because all that stuff Kye had just told me about his mom? Pretty much explained the surliness. He was basically a guy who was hurting. Who'd spent a lifetime hurting by the sound of it.

"You finished?" The corners of his mouth tilted, hinting at a smile.

"Asshole," I muttered, surprised by my urge to shove him again. "I'm honest with you and you're laughing at me?"

"Smiling. There's a difference." To prove it, he actually grinned, a fully-fledged, power-packed grin that left me feeling winded.

"Whatever." I shrugged and turned away, ready to admit defeat.

I'd wanted to step out of my comfort zone tonight, shake things up a little. But I wasn't ready to sign on as some guy's dumping ground. I wasn't a sadist.

I'd wanted to have fun tonight. To push my usual boundaries. To cut loose after a very long year of good grades and good wholesome fun.

Simply, I wanted to be bad.

"Stay."

I halted mid-step. Kye had spoken so softly I wondered if I'd conjured up his monosyllabic plea.

"Please," he added.

I bit back my first sarcastic response of 'who knew, the badass has manners' when I glanced over my shoulder and saw his expression.

Tortured. Mingled with fear and hope.

The hope is what convinced me.

If Kye hoped I'd hang around a little longer, I would. Not because I was some bimbo who'd do anything to break free of my rigid life. But because that expression on his face made me realize that the tough guy hid his vulnerabilities behind anger and a snide mouth. And I knew what it was like to hide behind a practiced front.

"Okay, I'll stay."

This time, his genuine smile made something in my chest twist.

Maybe I should've left after all.

FOUR
KYE

I had no idea why I asked the uptight princess to stay.

I should've let her stomp off in a snit after her shitfit.

But there was something about the way she'd stood up to me that had me intrigued.

I'd bet my left ball she was daddy's little angel. She'd virtually confirmed it when she'd blurted all that stuff about her private life.

So her tough girl act, when she'd shoved me around, made me admire her. She had spirit. Fire in the belly, as my mum used to say.

But I couldn't afford to think about Mum now. Not when Mia stared at me with those all-seeing, all-knowing eyes.

"Tell me why you want me to stay," she said, thrusting her chin up a little, daring me to drive her away again.

Considering she'd semi-lifted me out of my black mood, not a chance.

How long since I'd hung out with anyone, let alone a girl? After I'd been booted out of the tennis academy in Sydney for busting that bozo's nose, I'd spent a month at my dad's mansion in Double Bay, on what he'd labeled a good behavior bond.

Hadn't been so bad, as my dad was on location shooting an action flick in Darwin for three of those weeks. And that final week, he'd made arrangements for me to come here.

Woop-de-fucking-do.

"Honestly?"

She rolled her eyes. "Wouldn't have asked if I didn't want an honest answer."

I stepped forward, almost invading her personal space. "I've been in a pretty shitty place lately and you've distracted me."

"So you want me to stick around and distract you some more." She pressed her palms to her heart. "Lucky me."

"I also like that you're a smart-arse."

"I love your accent." Her lips curved into a sexy grin that made me want to step even closer. "Arrrrse," she said, and giggled.

I found myself chuckling along with her. "Let me guess. Your only experience with Australia comes from drooling over the Hemsworth brothers."

To my surprise, she blushed. "I may have seen The Hunger Games five times." She held up both hands, fingers spread. "And The Avengers ten. What of it?"

"Means you've got a thing for Aussie guys." I bumped her with my shoulder. "Lucky me."

She wrinkled her nose, but her blush intensified, making me want to touch her cheeks to see if they felt as hot as they looked. "You'll be the exception to the rule."

"Yet you're here with me now instead of at that party?" I grinned. "Interesting."

Our gazes locked for a long moment and I felt a jolt of something ... powerful. I could attribute it to hormones, considering I hadn't got laid in six months, but the spark in her dark eyes made me want to do more than chat with her.

She blinked and the moment vanished. "Already told you, I would've done anything to escape that party."

"Know the feeling." I glanced at her arms, knowing she wasn't a tennis player by the lack of muscle definition. "Considering I'm new at the academy, I had to be there. What's your excuse?"

"Family obligation." She shrugged, but I glimpsed tension flattening her lips. "You're a player?"

"Guilty as charged." I performed a fake serve. "Don't hold it against me."

Her gaze slid over me and my cock hardened. "You don't look like a player."

"I think you just insulted my muscles."

The faintest pink stained her cheeks again. "I meant your clothes." She gestured toward the clubhouse. "You don't look like the dweebs that hang around there in their Sunday school best."

"Thanks. I think." Funny, she'd echoed my thoughts from the brief time I'd spent at that party.

"You're aiming for grand slams?"

The million-dollar question. A few months ago, I would've said yes. I knew I was being fast-tracked for the APT after putting in good performances on the pro tour. Even though I was older than most rookies and had missed out on the bulk of the junior tour, the coaches kept pushing me.

Until I'd screwed up.

According to my dad, Dirk Cresswell had a reputation for turning careers around, hence my last ditch stand.

Problem was, did I want it? I'd lost the hunger lately.

But if I couldn't make it in tennis, what other options did I have?

"Tough question?"

I shook my head. "Just not sure how to answer it anymore."

The spark was back in her eyes, as if she found me infinitely fascinating. "I thought the slams were the ultimate dream of every tennis jock?"

I pointed at my clothes. "Thought we'd already established I'm not your average jock."

"No, you're not," she said so softly I barely heard her. "It's why I'm still here talking to you and not back in my villa with Liam or Chris."

I laughed. "You know I'll think less of you if you have Hemsworth cardboard cut-outs?"

She swiped at her brow. "Phew, your opinion of me is safe. I meant DVDs."

I liked how she answered me back. It made her more interesting. "So is it the muscles, the blue eyes, the height or the accent that has you hooked?"

"All of the above." She mocked a little swoon.

I leaned closer, enjoying the way her lips parted and her breathing became shallower. "I have all those attributes, but I don't see you swooning over me."

I expected her to step away. To elbow me.

Instead, she turned her head so our lips were inches apart. "The night is young, who knows what may happen later?"

I held my breath, reigning in the urge to kiss her. Not from some misplaced chivalry but because this was the first time in a long time I'd actually interacted with a girl on a level that didn't include a make-out session, a condom and a quick goodbye.

I may not kiss her but that didn't mean I couldn't flirt a little. "Is that a promise?"

Her mouth kicked up into a naughty smile that made me regret my impulse not to kiss her. "Only if you promise to catch me when I swoon."

"Deal." I winked and she groaned.

"Don't do the wink thing," she said. "Jocks do that all the time and think it's cool."

"Bet you wouldn't complain if the Hemsworths did it."

She poked me in the chest and swear I felt that brief contact all the way down to my soles. "The way you keep harping, I think you've got a thing for them too."

I held up my hands, enjoying our banter. "Nothing wrong with admiring a guy's craft and they're good actors."

Wondering how far I could push her, I lowered my tone. "Do you need proof I'm into girls and not guys?"

Her eyes widened and I glimpsed a beguiling mix of fear and anticipation.

Damn, it would be fun to make this good girl bad, even for a few hours.

"What did you have in mind?" she said, her gaze fixing on my mouth before sliding up to meet my eyes again.

"Babe, you don't want to know."

I threw it out there, curious to see what she'd do. I knew what I wanted her to do. Jump me, wrap those long bare legs around my waist, and ride me until dawn.

"What if I do?" Her tongue flicked out to moisten her lips and it almost undid my resolution to stay hands off.

I needed to cool this down fast, before flirting became fucking.

"You don't strike me as the one night stand type," I said, deliberately easing away and putting some distance between us.

"Now who's judging who?" she spat, her shoulders rigid with anger. "You don't have a clue what I want."

If this was one of those cartoons I used to love watching with Mum when I was a kid, Mia would have steam shooting out her ears, she looked that riled. Guess I touched a sore spot. Which made me wonder ...

"You're a virgin?"

"Hell no!" She crossed her arms and glowered in a fair imitation of one. "I just want ... um, I want ... uh, crap." She shook her head and turned away. "Forget it."

I should. But I didn't like seeing her revert to uptight so I asked the one question I shouldn't.

"What do you want?"

When she didn't answer, I grabbed her arm and gently tugged her to face me again. "Tell me."

She dragged her gaze from my chest, which she'd been studying with intent, to finally look at me. "I want to cut loose."

She sounded so forlorn I wanted to hug her. But if Mia ended up in my arms I wouldn't be able to stop at comforting.

"By graffiti-ing the club house? By carving your initials into the grass courts with a lawn mower? By unstringing all the rackets—"

"By having sex with you," she said, sounding soft and uncertain and embarrassed.

"Fuck me," slipped out before I had a second to come up with a more suitable response.

Her smile wobbled. "That's what I was hoping for."

I shook my head. "I didn't mean it like that." I dragged my hand through my hair. "You just threw me, that's all."

"Good, because that's how you've made me feel since

the minute we started talking." She drew in a deep breath and huffed it out. "Look, I never do this kind of thing."

"Even at college?"

She winced. "I'm kinda a nerd so no, I don't do dorm-hopping."

"So why me? Why tonight?"

I wanted her to articulate a reason, any reason, that I could throw back in her face as to why we couldn't do this. Because my dumb-arse libido? Already had her stripped with me deep inside her.

"Because you're hot," she blurted, and I laughed at her honesty.

"Thanks."

"And I want to step out of my comfort zone for once in my life."

I nodded. "So I was right at the start. Good girl wants to slum it for a while."

She reared back a little, as if I'd slapped her. "I wouldn't be slumming it. You're ... you're ... incredible."

I could've sworn my heart stopped beating at that moment. I couldn't breathe.

No one, apart from Mum, had ever looked at me the same way Mia was looking at me.

Like she could see the good stuff deep inside I hid from everyone.

Like she wanted to know more.

Like I was worthy.

And damn if it didn't harden my resolve all the more.

"I'm not even close to who you think I am," I said, shaking my head. "I'm a moody, arrogant prick."

"Yeah, keep telling yourself that." Her lopsided smile made something in my chest ache. "Maybe if you keep saying it long enough, you'll start to believe your own badass press."

There she went again, making me want to laugh.

"We've known each other for less than an hour." I held up my hands to ward her off. "You shouldn't want to sleep with an arsehole like me."

"Well too damn bad, because I do."

Before I could react, she'd flung herself on me, moving so fast my back slammed against the wire fence surrounding the court.

Her mouth crushed mine in an inexperienced meld of lips and teeth that had me tasting blood a second before she pushed away.

"Shit, I'm so sorry." She stared at my mouth. "You're bleeding."

I couldn't stand her shattered expression. "My first sex wound. Cool."

When she didn't lose the wide-eyed horror, I did the dumbest thing since I'd smashed that jerk's nose back in Sydney.

I reached for her and hauled her into my arms. "Just means you'll have to kiss it better."

"I'm no good at this." She sounded on the verge of tears. "Just forget it—"

I kissed her. Grazing my lips over hers. Repeatedly. Deepening the pressure with every pass until her mouth opened. My tongue slipped in, touched hers and I lost it.

I ravaged her mouth. Long, deep, hot kisses that made my cock ache.

She moaned when I groped her butt and pulled her flush against me, her thighs parting so I fit snug.

Damn, there was no fucking way this could stop at a kiss.

I wrenched my mouth from hers with difficulty. "Mia, we can't—"

"Ssh." She pressed a finger against my lips. "As much as I like hearing that accent, right now I want something else."

She ground her pelvis against my cock. "This."

When she did it again, slower this time, sliding up and down against me, I knew I was a goner.

FIVE
MIA

Trust me to pick the only bad boy on the planet with a conscience.

I didn't know what else to do to get Kye to sleep with me, bar strip and run around the tennis court naked.

"This isn't a good idea," he mumbled, sounding as tortured as I felt.

Good. Because if we didn't do this within the next five minutes, I'd combust from wanting him.

I pressed against him one last time, wishing I had the guts to touch him there. "We either do this, or you're going to spend the night under a cold shower or working off your frustration on the court."

The moment I said it, I had an idea. A brilliant one.

Trying to hide a triumphant smirk was almost impossible. "How about this. We play one game of tennis. I win, we have sex. You win, we don't."

His eyes narrowed, sizing me up. "You said you played badly, so what's the catch?"

"No catch." I shrugged, mustering my best innocent expression. "Come on. What have you got to lose?"

Apart from the game, because if there's one thing I knew about tennis, it was how to not play fair. I was average on the court. But I'd once watched Dani bring a guy to his knees by seducing him one shot at a time.

Now it was my turn to see if I had what it took to distract a gun player long enough that he fudged four points so we ended up in bed.

"You're giving in too easily." He shook his head. "I don't trust you."

"Shouldn't that be my line?" I smiled and flipped the catch on the storage box tucked outside the fence.

"Fine, we'll play one game, then I'm heading to bed," he muttered, rummaging through the rackets before he found one he fancied: testing the weight in his hand, fiddling with the strings, inspecting it.

"That's what I'm hoping for," I murmured, flashing him a smug grin when he glared at me.

He tapped the racket against his opposite palm. "You're not exactly dressed for tennis," he said, his gaze sliding over my high heels and bare legs, averting before he got any higher.

"Neither are you." I shrugged, slipped off my heels and kicked them away. "There. I'm ready."

He swore under his breath before shrugging out of his sports jacket and tossing it over the storage box.

I grabbed the first racket I could find and didn't even glance at it, earning another suspicious stare from Kye.

"You serve." I tossed him a few balls, which he caught deftly in one hand.

"Then this is going to be over faster than you think," he said, a flicker of a smile playing about his sexy mouth, the mouth I couldn't wait to kiss again. "They don't call me Ace for nothing."

I mimed chattering with my hand. "Too much of this."

He laughed. "Fine. Let's get this over with."

I blew him a kiss, not surprised he frowned, before I strutted toward my end of the court, wiggling my ass for all its worth.

He swore again.

I turned to face him, delighting in his tortured expression across the net. Holding my racket in both hands, I stretched overhead, reaching for the sky. His groan wasn't unexpected, considering my mini rode high enough to flash my white satin thong.

His first serve went wide.

"Fault," I yelled, complete with a fist pump in the air that made my dress ride up again.

The next ball flew at me so hard I would've bruised if it'd hit. As it was, it missed the service line by a foot.

"Double fault." I chalked up a point in the air to me. "Love, fifteen."

I saw his jaw clench in response as he stalked toward the other side of the court to serve again.

He glared at me across the net so I did what a girl in my position had to do. I unzipped my dress from collarbone to navel, grateful I'd listened to Dani and worn the sluttiest thing I owned.

"Fuck," he grunted, serving the softest ball I'd faced my entire life.

I slammed it back down the line with the best forehand I'd ever done. "I do believe that's love-thirty," I said, taking my spot on the other side of the court and bouncing on the balls of my feet, fully aware what affect that would have on my boobs.

He stared at the jiggling and scowled. "You're not playing fair."

Tossing my hair over my shoulder, I said, "I'm playing to win."

To prove it, I slid the zip lower.

He served. Wide.

I jumped up and down, and watched his eyes bug out of his head.

He double faulted again.

"Match point," I said, deliberately wiping make-believe sweat from my cleavage. Then repeating the action across my lower belly, just above the thong's elastic.

His next serve practically dribbled over the net and I lobbed it back over his head. He could've returned the shot. He didn't, considering he'd already flung his racket away and was stalking toward me with determination.

"I won," I said, licking my suddenly dry lips, as my heart threatened to leap out of my chest.

What the hell was I doing, taunting a guy like Kye into having sex with me?

"Babe, we're both about to be winners," he said, vaulting the net, hauling me into his arms and kissing me senseless.

When his hands slid lower, brushing past my breasts, touching the bare skin on my belly, I sagged against him. Bombarded by sensations. Wanting his hands all over me.

"Time to collect my winnings," I whispered against the corner of his mouth.

He eased back, the heat in his stare making my skin prickle. "I've never been so happy to get beat."

"Prove it."

He zipped me up, slid his hand into mine, and we sprinted toward his villa.

SIX
KYE

This was a bad idea.

Mia might talk the talk but in the morning I had no doubt she'd walk the walk ... of shame.

She'd regret having sex with me. Not that I could tell by looking at her now as I kicked the villa door shut and she hauled me closer.

"Want to know a secret?" Her lips curved into a knowing smile that had me balling my hands into fists to stop from ripping her clothes off.

"You're secretly engaged to Liam Hemsworth?"

"I wish." She stood on tiptoe and brushed her lips against mine. "No, my secret is far more nefarious."

I smiled against her mouth. "Use smaller words please. I'm just an Aussie tennis jock, remember?"

She placed her palms on my chest and pushed gently. "I knew you didn't stand a chance once I started stripping on the court."

She shimmied for emphasis and I couldn't help staring at her pert tits again, jiggling over the top of a white lace bra. "You could've been Nadal and Dokovic rolled into one and I still would've had you." She snapped her fingers. "Just like that."

"For a self-confessed nerd, you're pretty ballsy." I rested my hands on her waist and backed her toward the sofa. "Guess it's time to show you what winners get."

Her knees buckled as they hit the sofa cushions and I eased her backward until she lay sprawled before me, that damn zipper tag still toying with her navel.

So I knelt and did what I'd been dying to do since I'd first seen her in that dress. I grabbed the zipper tab and yanked it all the way down.

The dress fell away, leaving her lithe, tanned body on display. Smooth skin. Small waist. Flared hips. B cup.

Breathtaking.

"You're staring," she said, squirming slightly.

"That's because you're beautiful." I dipped my head and licked the tempting skin in the curve of her waist. She tasted as good as she looked.

She giggled. "That tickles."

Her natural response made me pause. There was an inherent innocence about Mia. She may not be a virgin but I'd bet my left nut she wasn't far off it. I didn't go for the naive type and never had sex with them. Led to too many complications: expectations, ruminations, recriminations.

But with Mia lying before me, her big brown eyes alight with passion, I couldn't back out now. Though I could appease my conscience one last time.

"You're sure about this?"

"For fuck's sake," she muttered, surging upward to drape her arms around my neck. "Yes, Kye, I'm sure."

Her death grip on me softened as she lowered her hands to grab the end of my T-shirt. "I want you."

She peeled the T-shirt off and flung it away, her gaze as

greedy as her hands as she touched my chest, my abs. *"Now."*

When her fingers skimmed the waistband of my jeans, I growled and shoved her back down on the sofa.

Her soft body felt good beneath me and as I ground my hips against hers, she moaned in a way that made me want to pleasure her all night.

"You feel good," she said, as I kissed her ear, sucking the fleshy lobe into my mouth, biting down on it. "And whatever you're doing with your mouth, don't stop."

"I'm betting you'll be screaming that real soon," I murmured in her ear, as I trailed kisses down her neck, across her collarbone, across her tits.

She arched, offering herself to me, and I slid my hands behind her back, flicked her bra hooks and ripped the scrap of white lace off.

Dark pink areola. Rock hard nipples. Gorgeous.

I sucked one into my mouth, the ache in my cock intensifying as she started writhing. Fuck, if she was this responsive with a little foreplay, I couldn't wait to see her get off.

I alternated between her nipples: nibbling, licking, sucking. Until we were both pretty mindless.

I needed to be inside her. Now.

I resumed kneeling, hooked my thumbs under the elastic of her thong and peeled it off.

She watched me, her eyes widening when I insinuated myself between her ankles and eased her legs apart.

Slick, wet heaven.

I bent forward, eager to taste her, but she placed her hand on my forehead.

"Uh ... Kye? I've never done ... what I mean is, you ... down there—"

Incredulous, I stared up at this amazing woman willing

to have sex with me when she'd never had a guy go down on her. "You've never been given head before?"

She shook her head, gnawing on her bottom lip. "I hate that I'm inexperienced at this stuff—"

"Babe, after tonight, you won't be."

With that, I leaned forward and swiped my tongue against her clit. She bucked.

"Easy." I lightly held her hips as my tongue swirled and nipped and sucked, while Mia went a little crazy.

I swore it took less than a minute when she came with a yell that made me smile.

Nothing sexier than an uninhibited woman. And for someone with little sexual experience, it made it all the sexier that she responded to me like that.

"That was ..." —she stared at me with adoration— "fricking unbelievable."

"And to think, we're only just getting started." I stood, unsnapped the button on my jeans and eased the zip down.

"Faster," she demanded, her tongue darting out to moisten her bottom lip as her gaze riveted to my zip.

"For the first time, maybe." I slid the jeans and my boxers down at the same time, enjoying her gasp and gaping mouth. "But just so you know, when we do this again in the bedroom soon, we'll be going real slow."

She nodded, mute, as she tentatively reached for me. When her fingers closed around my cock, a vice clamped my head.

I had to be inside her.

As she slid her hand up and down my shaft slowly, then cupped my balls, I grabbed my wallet out of my jeans, fished out the condom and ripped the foil as fast as I could.

"Babe, you're killing me." I stilled her hand and rolled

the condom on. "If I'm not inside you within the next five seconds this party will be over before it's begun."

"You like me touching you?" Her smile wobbled, making me want to hold her close.

Damn it, this is why I didn't do vulnerable. I did fast and furious sex. Something I needed to focus on before I let a woman I barely knew creep under my guard; more than she already had. In one fucking night.

"Yeah, you can touch all you want. Later." I lowered myself onto her, liking the skin-to-skin contact as my cock nudged her pussy. "For now, this is where I want to be."

I slid into her. Tight heat gripped me. Squeezed me. Engulfed me.

Perfection.

Then I started moving, in and out, hard and fast. I needed this. Needed to be in a beautiful woman who wanted me as badly as I wanted her. Needed to banish the loneliness. Needed to forget. Everything.

"Oh my God, Kye, you feel so good ..." She wrapped her legs around my waist and I drove into her harder. "Oh yeah, just like that ..."

I wanted to kiss her, craved it like a thirsty man in the dessert, but I wanted to watch her come more, so I slipped a hand between our bodies and fingered her clit.

Her gaze locked on mine, wide and wondrous, as I changed the angle slightly and pounded deeper.

"Kye, please..." she begged, her arse lifting off the sofa as the pressure built and instinct took over.

I slammed into her and she met me thrust for thrust, the strength of my orgasm almost making me black out as she screamed my name.

As we both came back down to earth, I searched for the

right words, any words, to convey how monumentally phenomenal that was.

Until I realized something. I never dwelled on the right thing to say after sex with other girls. My post-coital conversation consisted of a thanks and a see you later. Which never eventuated.

I didn't do involvement and I never emotionally connected with anyone.

So why the fuck did having sex with Mia make me feel like I'd just done both?

SEVEN
MIA

Speechless, I stared at Kye's chest.

Because maybe if I kept looking at it long enough, the right words would form in my head and I might have a remote chance in hell of articulating something, anything, other than WTF?

If what I'd just done with Kye was sex, those other few times? A lackluster preview before the main performance.

What he'd done with his mouth ... and the rest ...

Heat scorched my cheeks. Yeah, like a blush meant anything now. The guy was still inside me, for goodness sake.

"Be back in a sec."

But not for long, as he slid out and headed for the bathroom. Leaving me with a sensational view of the best ass I'd ever seen and a distinct case of 'what the hell do I do now?'

I heard the shower running and contemplated following him in there for one insane second before dismissing it as PTSD: Post Terrific Sex Ditziness.

First things first, I couldn't be sprawled naked on his

sofa when he returned so I sat up, grabbed my dress and shrugged into it.

I was fumbling with the zip when he strolled into the lounge, a towel knotted at his hip.

"The shower's all yours if you want it," he said, gesturing at the bathroom. "I'll make us something to eat."

It all sounded so normal, so nice, if not for the fact he could barely look me in the eye.

I could take the easy option and scuttle for the bathroom, drown out my thoughts beneath the showerhead, then pretend like we hadn't had mind-blowing sex.

But what I was feeling? A confusing jumble of awe, affection and serious lust—the latter most of all—meant I needed to confront Kye before things got really awkward. Besides, I was hoping for an encore later.

"Kye?"

He paused at the door to his bedroom and glanced over his shoulder, his expression shuttered. "Yeah?"

"That was amazing."

The tension compressing his lips eased and they curved into a semi smile that made me feel warm and gooey inside. "So I lived up to your Hemsworth fantasies?"

"The only person I was thinking about that whole time was you." And I meant it. By the shock widening his eyes, maybe articulating it wasn't such a good idea, but I'd never been a game player.

I didn't flirt or simper or pretend. When I liked a guy I told him. Which probably accounted for my pathetic track record with men.

"Same here, babe."

Our gazes locked across the room, sparking the air between us with something indefinable, before he turned away and strode into the bedroom.

Thankfully, he didn't close the door and I watched him drop the towel and pull on a pair of sweats and a T-shirt. Damn, if Kye looked hot in clothes, he was stunning naked. The muscle definition, the hardness, the tan ... that didn't extend to certain parts I'd been privy to see.

I'd had sex with a tennis jock I barely knew.

Freaking hell.

I pressed my palms to my hot cheeks. Yeah, like that would cool them down. Maybe a shower wasn't a bad idea. A cold one.

I leaped off the sofa and headed for the bathroom, needing to restore some normality to this otherwise crazy night. I loved hot showers, the longer the better. I did some of my best thinking under the spray. And that's what I needed to do now, come up with a flippant yet genuine way to extricate myself from Kye's villa before I did something stupid: like move in.

"Lame," I muttered, stripping my dress off and fiddling with the taps until the water temp was just right.

I stepped inside the large cubicle, specially built for the tennis jocks that stayed in these villas, closed my eyes and tipped my head back under the water stream. Bliss.

Humming some soppy ballad from a rom-com I'd seen last semester, I turned my face to the spray, the sharp peppering of the water giving me the wake up call I needed.

You've just had a one night stand.

You should leave, not hang around showering and eating a meal he's whipping up out of obligation.

I groaned and resisted bashing my head against the tiles, just. And that's when the shower door creaked open and I felt a pair of hands clasp my waist, before sliding upward to rest under my breasts.

"Need some help getting clean?" Kye whispered in my

ear, pulling my back flush against his front.

Wow.

Banishing my sensible, good girl thoughts of leaving ASAP, I turned in the circle of his arms. "Don't you mean dirty?"

The wicked quirk to his lips made my heart pound in anticipation as he lowered his head and kissed me. Slow. Sensual. Deep. The type of kiss that could make a girl forget everything but being naked and wet with a guy like Kye.

I was on sensation overload, with his hands massaging my ass, the water pounding my back and his mouth wreaking havoc. When we came up for air, I could barely stand.

"I thought you were cooking?"

"I couldn't stay away." He stared into my eyes and rested his forehead on mine. "I don't do this usually."

"Shower?" I wrinkled my nose. "Euw. Now you tell me."

He didn't smile, his solemnity at odds with the passion darkening his eyes to indigo. "I'm not a man whore but I've had my fair share of sex. Sex that ends the minute we finish fucking."

A sliver of something akin to jealousy lanced my gut. "Is that my cue to leave?"

"No." The monosyllable exploded out of him.

"That's just it." He closed his eyes, dragged in a breath and ducked his head under the water spray before refocusing on me.

"I want you to stay." He cupped my face in his hands. "I want to fuck you in this shower and in the kitchenette and in the bed." He searched my face, as if looking for answers. "Does that sound insane?"

In response, I hooked a leg around his waist and rotated my hips against him, real slow. "Let the madness begin."

And we did go a little nuts. My first fully-fledged sexathon. We did it in the shower. On the lounge room floor. On his bed. On the tiny island bench in the kitchen. Insatiable. Hedonistic. Beyond memorable.

I didn't sleep. I couldn't, not with my body humming from overuse and my mind buzzing with so many questions, the main one being would Kye be open to continuing this fling for the duration?

I was under no illusions that this was nothing more than sex, but somewhere between shoving popcorn into each other's mouths after our bench-top performance and cuddling beneath the sheets, I envisaged this being the grand vacation romance I'd never had.

At dawn, I gave up trying to sleep. Instead, I watched Kye: the way his eyelashes created fan shadows on his cheeks, the way he puffed out air every second breath, the way he looked young and carefree, at odds with the carefully controlled tension he'd exhibited last night.

I liked this guy.

But was the feeling mutual?

Too wired to watch him and ponder any longer, I slipped out of bed, got dressed and headed for the door. Besides, I needed to make it back to my villa before the early risers started heading for the courts.

Not that I was ashamed of hooking up with Kye but I knew how the rumor mill worked in this place. I'd lived here long enough to see girls' reputations shredded, no matter if they were groupies or not.

The last thing I needed was for my dad to give me grief. Or worse, give Kye grief.

For now, I'd keep this under wraps.

And figure out what the hell I was going to do about my crazy crush on a sexy Aussie I hardly knew.

EIGHT
KYE

I followed my usual warm up routine. Calf stretches. Hamstrings. Quads. Hip flexors, before moving onto my back, my pecs, triceps and biceps.

Usually I was one hundred percent focused on my body during a warm up, deriving comfort from the familiar sting of muscle that eased away as it elongated.

Not today. Today, all I could think about was Mia.

The sounds she made when she came. The way she'd tasted. The way she'd looked with her mouth wrapped around my cock.

Fuck.

I dropped into a squat and breathed deep, evenly, willing my hard-on to vanish.

When I'd envisaged icebergs for a full two minutes I stood, to find Miles, my workout partner, tapping his palm against his racket, testing string tension.

"Hey, Down Under. Ready to get whipped again?"

I'd never had a nickname before, one that wasn't douchebag or prick from the lowlifes that frequented Mum's club, so I didn't mind Miles constantly ribbing me about everything from my accent to Vegemite to shrimps on the barbie.

"Big talk to compensate for a little dick perhaps, mate?" I picked up my racket and bounced it from hand to hand, taking comfort in the familiar feel of it. "Because by the amount of crap you spout, Miles my man, you must be about this big." I held up my thumb and forefinger an inch apart.

Miles guffawed. "I'm going to whip your Aussie ass good."

"Bring it on, little fella." I wiggled my drooping pinkie under his nose.

I joined in his laughter as we chose balls and headed for the court. Maybe a good hit out would clear my head. And boy, did it need to be cleared.

All I could think about was Mia. About what we'd done and what I'd like to do again. And that's what was throwing me the most. Bad enough I'd spent the entire night with her. I wanted more. More nights like last one. Laughing and teasing and feeling good about myself for the first time in forever.

I should've been glad she'd bolted when I woke. Instead, I'd acted like some needy chick, rolling over and burying my face in her pillow just so I could smell her.

Yep. I definitely needed to smash a few balls around to work off this antsy feeling that made me want to ditch Miles and go find Mia.

"What did you think of the party?" Miles paused to lace up his shoe.

"Not my scene."

Miles straightened, his smug grin grating. "Saw you leave with Mia."

I stiffened, not liking the way Miles said her name. How crazy was that? "So?"

"Be careful there, bro." Miles slapped me on the back. "Dirk may be a pretty cool guy but fuck with his daughter? He'll castrate you."

I stared at Miles as the truth detonated.

Mia was Dirk Cresswell's daughter.

Fuck, fuck, fuck.

The familiar fury bubbled up at the injustice of every single thing in my life going wrong.

What made this worse? Being with Mia felt so right.

I wanted to smash something. My racket. The net. The fence. Kick and pound and belt out the frustration making my insides clench with the unfairness of it.

But I did none of those things.

No more outbursts from me, not any more. I might not regret busting that pansy-arse's nose back in Sydney, but seeing his blood on my knuckles had been a wake up call.

I couldn't let the anger beat me. So I had to beat it.

Forcing a smile that felt like my face was cracking, I gestured at the court. "Thanks for the tip, mate, but isn't it time you stopped gossiping like an old woman and let me teach you a lesson?"

"You're all talk, Down Under," Miles yelled, as he jogged to his side of the court and flipped me the bird.

I wish I was all talk. Instead, last night I'd been all action and what I'd done with Mia may have cost me my final chance at having a tennis career.

I was so screwed.

NINE
MIA

"I sussed out your bad boy," Dani said, topping up her OJ. "The rumor mill is working overtime."

My heart froze. How could anyone know about last night? I'd been so careful doing the walk of shame back to my villa. No one had seen me. Had they? Shit.

Channeling disinterest, I poured more coffee. "What are people saying?"

Dani waggled her finger at me. "Uh-uh. No way am I telling you a thing 'til you spill what happened last night when you left the party."

She leaned close. "Did you do him?"

Unable to keep the smile off my face at the memory of how well I'd 'done' Kye, I shrugged and feigned nonchalance. "Maybe."

Dani squealed and slugged me on the arm. "You did! I'm so proud of you, hon."

Slathering peach jelly on my toast, I said, "I'm not telling you another thing 'til I hear these rumors."

"Fine." Dani slumped in her chair and fake pouted.

"Apparently he was a wunderkind in Oz. Big things expected of him. 'Til he got into a fight with another player at their top academy, beat him to a pulp and was kicked out."

My heart sank. Kye may have given off bad boy vibes initially last night but to be that aggressive? He'd mentioned breaking his hand by smashing some dude's windshield too. Didn't bode well that he'd been expelled from his tennis academy for violence also.

Dani slipped a silver flask out of her carry all and added a dash of what I knew to be vodka to her OJ. "No one wanted to know him in Oz but your dad somehow heard about him and offered him a place here." She sipped at her vodka-pepped OJ and sighed with pleasure. "It's his last chance."

Ah hell.

Kye would freak when he found out the guy who'd given him another chance was her dad.

"Which makes me wonder ..." Dani tapped her bottom lip with a crimson manicured nail. "If you slept with the bad boy, it means you like him. And presuming the sex was phenomenal by the glow and goofy grin you can't wipe off your face, you want a repeat. But is loverboy happy doing the boss's daughter?"

That's what I intended to find out.

I grimaced and Dani clapped a hand over her mouth. "Oh my God. You didn't tell him!"

"It didn't come up," I said, knowing that wouldn't cut it with Kye.

I'd deliberately omitted my last name when I'd introduced myself to him because I knew he would've ditched me the second I uttered Cresswell as my surname.

It had happened too many times before, unless the guys trying to chat me up were Dad's suck-ups, jocks who'd do anything—including play nice with me—to get in the good graces of their boss and idol.

"I bet that's not what you said to the bad boy later." Dani winked and downed her doctored OJ in four gulps. "I'm sure he got it up—"

"Stop it." My rebuke came out harsher than intended and Dani's over made-up eyes for this hour of the morning widened.

"What's biting your ass?"

"I just don't want to dissect what happened with Kye, okay?" And particularly not in the lewd, crude way Dani expected.

I loved my best friend, I really did, but after not seeing her for a few semesters, her brash, in-your-face innuendo for all things sexual really grated.

I thought Kye and I had really connected last night. And I wanted to see him again. If anything, to have a chance to explain why I didn't tell him who I was. But it was more than that. Simply, no guy had ever made me feel how I felt with him.

Kye may be tough on the outside but I'd seen glimpses of an inner softness that drew me to him on some weird, intrinsic level.

"Fine," Dani said, but I glimpsed the fleeting hurt in her eyes and damned if I didn't know how to make it better. "Though this guy isn't one of your fixer-uppers. Sounds like he's way past that."

I bristled. "You don't know anything about him, bar a few shitty rumors."

"And you do?" Dani arched an eyebrow, managing to look superior and condescending at the same time.

I bit back my first response of 'I know a lot more than you.'

Like how he liked his ass gripped when he was inside me. Like how his eyes turned almost black the moment before he came. Like how he made me feel like a woman for the first time in my life. A feeling I'd give anything to recapture.

"In case you hadn't noticed, I'm here on vacation," I said, doing my best to remain cool when I wanted to leap from the table and stalk back to my villa. "So I'm having a little fun. No harm in that."

Dani tsk-tsked. "Sweetie, I've known you a long time. Long enough to have seen you want to nurture wounded birds, stray dogs and moody dudes." She tapped me on the nose. "You're a fixer upper. It's what you do. It's sweet but delusional, because with some guys, no matter how many hard yards you put in, they'll never change."

"You make me sound like a gullible idiot," I muttered, twisting the napkin in my lap to prevent from wringing my BFF's neck.

Her expression softened. "That's not what I'm saying."

"Then what?"

"You're a pushover, sweetie. Too soft-hearted for your own good and I don't want you investing time and effort in any guy who doesn't deserve it."

I could've accepted Dani's advice if not for one salient fact. She was the queen of wasting time on guys who didn't deserve her attention let alone anything else.

I nodded. "Wise advice." I tempered what I was about to say with a smile. "You should adhere to it some time."

She waved away my statement. "Doesn't apply to me, because I don't feel anything for the douchebags. Not in here." She pointed to her heart. "You, on the other hand?"

She picked up the butter knife and pretended to stab it into her chest. "Broken heart just waiting to happen."

I shook my head. "You're wrong."

Now if only I believed it.

TEN
KYE

After whipping Miles' arse on the practice court, I went in search of Mia.

We had to talk.

And she sure as hell wouldn't like what I had to say.

I didn't have to look far. When I headed back to my villa to change out of my sweaty gear, I saw her perched on the back step. And damned if my heart didn't give a betraying leap.

My *heart*? What the fuck was wrong with me? So we'd had sensational sex and talked a bit. Didn't mean I had to go all loopy.

The sooner we cleared the air and got things straight between us, the sooner Daddy's little princess could go back to her chino-wearing jocks and leave me the hell alone.

She stood as I neared, her eyes lighting up. Man, this was going to be tough.

"You shouldn't be here." I glanced over my shoulder, though I'd already scoped the surrounds to make sure no one was watching us.

"Good morning to you too," she said, the spark in her eyes fading. "Got beaten at practice?"

"Not bloody likely." I opened the back door and gestured her to enter in front of me. "We need to talk."

"You know," she said, her tone flat as she stepped past me and I gritted my teeth against the urge to bury my face in her fruity scented hair. "About my dad."

"Yeah." I flung my workout bag in the corner of the kitchenette. "What the fuck were you thinking?"

She spun on me so fast I backed into the wall. "I was *thinking* maybe you wanted to cut loose for a few hours last night."

She jabbed me in the chest with her index finger. "I was *thinking* you were attracted to me as much as I was attracted to you."

She stepped in real close, almost treading on my toes. "I was *thinking* you were the type who wouldn't give a rat's ass about a person's parents."

She stuck her face into mine, mere inches away. "Guess I was wrong."

I couldn't think with her so close, the tantalizing strawberry scent of her body wash or shampoo teasing my nostrils and making me want to imprint that smell on my skin again, the way it had last night.

I needed to push her away, to ensure she wouldn't come hanging around again and to do that, I'd need to give her some semblance of the truth.

Just frigging great.

"You weren't wrong," I said, ducking past her before I hauled her into my arms. "Drink?"

"No thanks." She crossed her arms and perched on the arm of the sofa. The same sofa we'd had sex on last night. A vivid image of the two of us flashed in my head. Not helping. "So what's your problem? You hanging out with me shouldn't change anything—"

"Bullshit." I grabbed a bottled water from the fridge, twisted the top off and chugged half of it. "You're not that naive. You must have some idea how pissed off your dad would be to find you with me."

I slammed the bottle down on the kitchen counter, spilling the remainder of the water. "Listen up, Princess, because I'm only going to say this once. I'm on my last chance here. Screw up and I'm done. No more tennis career. So the fact Dirk is your dad" —I shook my head— "it's a pretty big fucking deal."

Her shoulders slumped. "I'm twenty-one. I can date whoever I want."

My upper lip curled. "So tell me, how many tennis jocks have you dated that weren't handpicked by your old man?"

Her hesitation told me all I needed to know before she answered. "He wants me to be happy."

"As long as it's someone he approves of, right?" I thumped a fist against my chest. "Me? Your dear old dad would have a shitfit if he knew we'd hooked up last night. No fucking way would he approve of me."

Her mouth twisted into a stubborn grimace. "You don't know that. My dad's fair. He wouldn't have given you a spot here otherwise."

A derisive snort burst out of me. "The only reason your dad gave me a spot here is because my dad probably promised him a sizeable donation to expand the courts or clubhouse or whatever."

Her eyes narrowed. "You don't have a very high opinion of people, do you?"

"Let's just say where I'm from, I've seen it all. Mixed with all types. Rich or poor, educated or dumb-arses, people are mostly lying scum." I shrugged. "So excuse me for doubting your dad's motives for accepting me here."

I could almost see the wheels turning in her head as she thought up a suitable response to my bluntness. But I wasn't in the mood for any more of her trite platitudes. The sooner I stopped noticing the way her nipples were outlined beneath her tight red T shirt, or the way her denim mini ended mid-thigh, or the way she absentmindedly nibbled on her bottom lip when she was thinking, the better.

"Look, last night was great." I could've sworn her lower lip wobbled so I rushed on. "You're great, but I can't afford to piss off your dad and I need to focus on my tennis."

"So that's it?" She spoke too softly, too calmly. I didn't trust women when they were like this. My mum used to be the same when she was livid about something. The eerie calm usually preceded a shit-storm. "I don't get a say in any of this?"

"What's to say?" I'd have to be harsher to drive her away before I did something stupid, like relent. "You wanted a little walk on the wild side last night. You got it. I think you're hot and I took advantage of what you were offering. Let's just leave it at that."

She stood, even her posture unnaturally relaxed and calm. "What if I say no?"

"Fuck, Mia, what do you want from me?" I dragged my hand through my hair, a habit I thought I'd conquered a long time ago, around the time one of the bouncers at Mum's club in the Cross had whipped my arse for being a 'pansy'. Lessons like that stuck.

"I want us to be friends," she said, holding her hands out

to me like she had nothing to hide. "Discounting the sex last night, which we both know was amazing, I thought we connected."

She glanced away, as if nervous. "I don't have many friends in these parts anymore. Since I went away to college, I only vacation at home occasionally. Most of the tennis crowd who train here are transient and the rest are fake schmoozers who want to suck up to me to get to my dad." Her fingers clenched into fists. "I hate it."

"That's why you targeted me last night, wasn't it? Because I didn't look like one of your dad's hangers-on?"

She nodded. "I already told you that. But it was more ..." She wrinkled her nose. "You were partially right about me. All that stuff you said when we first met? I am daddy's little girl. It's been the two of us since Mom died. We're close and he's cool. But because we don't see each other much these days, when we do, he smothers me."

"So you think he'd approve of you being friends with a bum like me?"

"You're not a bum." Her lips curved into the smile I remembered from last night, the smile that could slay a guy and make him doing crazy things: like say fuck the altruistic crap and let's go to bed. "You're different."

"Which is why you targeted me in the first place."

"Yeah." Her gaze locked on mine, willing me to believe we could do this. "But then you started talking and that Aussie accent, plus the resemblance to the Hemsworths, did the rest."

"You're obsessed," I said, grinning like a loon and enjoying our reversion to teasing way too much to be good for me.

"Yeah, but not just with them." She walked across the

small lounge to lay a hand on my chest, directly over my heart. "I'll have a chat with my dad. Tell him we're friends. But that means we need to do some friendly stuff together."

"We got pretty friendly last night," I said, willing my heart to stop bucking like a wild thing beneath her palm.

To my surprise, and delight, she blushed. I didn't think girls did that any more. "Have you been to LA before?"

I shook my head. "Boys from the Cross don't get to travel much, let alone overseas. Every cent Mum earned was poured back into the club to keep it viable. And most of the money I earned went to her and to fund my tennis."

Surprisingly, she didn't ask questions or delve into my past. Brownie points for her.

"In that case, how would you like a guided tour of all the LA hot spots? Hollywood Boulevard. Melrose. Beverly Hills. The works." Her palm pressed harder against my chest. "It's what friends do. Hang out. Have fun."

I was tempted. Seriously tempted. I'd seen nothing of LA, bar the crazy freeways from LAX to Santa Monica. Hell, I hadn't even seen anything of the area surrounding the tennis academy.

"If I agree to this, we're just friends, okay?" I managed to keep a straight face while delivering the rest. "No funny business."

Her smile was radiant. "You thought what we did last night was funny?"

I waggled my finger under her nose. "And stop talking about it, okay?"

"Why?" Her gaze dipped to below my waist. "You have a boner?"

I stepped away before she could feel how right she was. "Friends don't talk to each other like that."

She hesitated, before nodding slowly. "Okay. Friends it is. I can do friends."

"Good, because it's all I'm offering, Mia."

It had to be, despite every instinct in my worthless body screaming to grab hold of this incredibly spirited girl and never let go.

ELEVEN
KYE

I didn't go for touristy stuff as a rule. Hated the rubberneckers who trawled the Cross, torn between gawking at the trannies and avoiding the hawkers trying to entice them into peep shows.

But the opportunity to see some of LA while I was here, especially through Mia's eyes, was too good to pass up.

I'd turned into a soft-cock when she'd given me that spiel about being friends. I shouldn't have bought into it. Should've made a firmer stand and kept my distance. Instead, we'd spent the last few hours visiting places I'd seen on TV: Rodeo Drive, Melrose, Sunset Strip, Kodak Theatre.

Interesting, but not half as interesting as the woman by my side. She'd recited funny anecdotes and teased and bumped me with her hip, like friends do. The decidedly unfriendly thoughts running through my head? Major pain in the arse.

Last stop was the Hollywood sign. Maybe I'd grow some balls and reiterate how this friends thing wasn't working for me.

It would kill me to do it, considering she'd been so nice to me tonight and hadn't crossed the line. The fact I wanted to leap so far over that frigging line wasn't helping.

"Shouldn't we be closer to the sign?"

She shook her head, not taking her eyes off the road. "It's not worth trekking up Mount Lee. The trails are tough and there's a razor-wire fence which means even if we did make the climb, we can't get within twenty feet of it."

"Seriously? Then that's the biggest piece of false advertising I've ever seen." I snorted. "Everyone thinks the Hollywood sign is LA. It's iconic. And you're telling me we can't even get near it?"

"Yep." She shot me a cheeky grin. "I'll make it up to you by throwing in my Santa Monica special tour."

"Let me guess. We can't get near the pier unless we swim with sharks?"

She chuckled. "Funny guy." She jerked her head toward the window. "Take a look. We're almost at the corner of Glen Holly and Beachwood Canyon Drive, which means you'll get to see your precious sign."

"But I want to get near it." At that moment I caught sight of the gigantic HOLLYWOOD sign and had to admit, it was impressive.

If the Sydney Harbor Bridge and Opera House defined Sydney for tourists, this sign was it for me in LA. I wouldn't forget my first glimpse of it. Especially as Mia had pulled over in a secluded spot, killed the engine and was currently staring at me with more than friendship in her eyes.

"No," I said, getting out of the car before I did something monumentally stupid, like hauling her into my lap.

She stepped out of the driver's side and followed me. "I didn't ask a question for you to refuse."

I sank onto a log and dropped my head into my hands. "You didn't have to. You're easier to read than a Penthouse."

She wrinkled her nose. "I thought we've had a nice evening. If you've read more into it than there is—"

"I may be many things, an idiot isn't one of them." I glared at her, wishing she'd show some reaction other than radiating calm, which only served to rile me further.

"Never said you were." She touched my knee and I jumped like she'd tasered me. "What's really wrong?"

It wouldn't do any good to articulate half the confusion I was feeling but odds were Mia had inherited her dad's persistence, the same dogged determination that had earned Dirk fifteen Grand Slams in a row.

"I'm having a hard time keeping my hands off you," I muttered, curling my fingers into my palms to stop from demonstrating. "The only option we have is to be friends but after last night ... what happened between us ..." I shook my head. "It's harder than I thought it'd be."

She patted my knee before removing her hand. It should've been a condescending gesture. Coming from Mia, it seemed comforting. "I get where you're coming from, wanting to be just friends. I'm a complication you don't need."

She sounded so forlorn I wanted to hug her. "If my dad has any say in it, this time next year you'll be on the ATP circuit, then it's the Slams after that."

Wish I had her confidence. "I haven't even done the pro tour yet, and that's the only way to earn early world ranking points."

"You're being fast-tracked if you're at Cresswell Academy." She turned to face me and I almost choked on my next breath. The admiration blazing from her steady gaze made me feel like I'd already won Wimbledon. "You think you're at the academy because your dad promised money to mine? Well, here's a newsflash, hotshot. My dad doesn't need money. And he wouldn't accept you just to settle an old score between buddies." She poked me in the chest. "My dad trains winners. Grand Slam winners. He wouldn't risk his reputation on anything less."

As Mia's heartfelt words sunk in, for the first time since I'd arrived in LA, I allowed myself to hope.

I wanted to play shit-hot tennis to repay my dad for the faith he'd shown in me over the last seven years, since he'd discovered I existed. He could've wimped out, considering I was a major pain in the arse. He didn't. And with my latest indiscretion, being booted out of Australia's number one academy, he'd really come through for me.

But what if I *was* good enough to satisfy my toughest critic, me?

"Thanks," I said, awkwardly reaching for her hand and grabbing it before I thought better of it. "Though you know you've just given me another reason why we can't be more than friends, right?"

She squeezed my hand, and held on tight. It felt fucking great. "I'm hoping once you get your head around the fact my dad sees you as a top tennis prospect and you've earned your spot, there may be room for me in your life too."

I swear my chest ached at her honesty. Not many women would take the risk of putting themselves out there, especially after I'd already dropkicked her heart. But I couldn't afford to waver. There was too much riding on this.

"Mia, we've only had one night together. How could you possibly want me in your life?"

My thumb absentmindedly traced circles on the back of her hand as I tried to formulate the words not to hurt her. "I'm not that much of a bastard to suggest what happened between us was a one night stand only, because we both know it went beyond that, but tennis is my life."

I drew in a deep breath and let it out. "It's all I have left."

Fuck, had I said that out loud? It's how I felt but I didn't need Mia seeing me at my most vulnerable. No one saw beneath my carefully cultivated tough guy image. Ever. So what was it about this woman that made me want to blurt my deepest, darkest secrets after knowing her twenty-four hours?

"What about your dad?" She sounded so sad—for me—I felt obliged to reassure her.

"We're not that close." I released her hand, knowing if I kept holding on, I'd never want to let go. "He's a mega TV star in Oz. Household name. Didn't know I existed 'til Mum died and her lawyer contacted him because it was stipulated in her will." I pinched the bridge of my nose. "She'd left the strip club to me but wanted Dad to be executor and manage it 'til I turned eighteen."

Her eyes widened. "You run a strip club?"

"Hell no." I scowled, not wanting to be reminded of the place that had ultimately cost Mum her life.

Not from the drugs or prostitution that was synonymous with Kings Cross, but from her dedication to proving she could be a *bona fide* businesswoman above the sleaze surrounding her. Ultimately, the manic hours she worked and her obsession with making money to provide a secure future for me had cost her. She'd dropped dead of a heart attack at forty-one. "Dad sold the club and invested the money for me. Sent me to boarding school 'til I turned eighteen, then I bought a small flat in Bondi with the cash."

"Sounds like your dad cares about you." Her severe stare held recrimination. "Which means you're far from alone."

"You wouldn't understand," I said, wishing I'd never

started down the road to deep and meaningful. "Your dad has probably adored you since the day you were born. Mine only does what he does out of obligation."

To her credit, she didn't try to dispute it. Instead, she gnawed on her bottom lip, a habit I happened to like, considering I got to stare at that lush, full lip and remember how it had tasted.

"You've had it tough but you're wrong, you're not alone," she said, daring me to disagree. "For as long as you're here in LA, you've got me."

My mouth curled into a reluctant smile, as I couldn't help but admire her tenacity. She'd be an amazing girlfriend. Loyal and protective and loving. Pity I'd never find out.

"So you're my new BFF, huh?"

"And don't you forget it." Her shoulder bumped mine and damned if I didn't want to blurt that I'd never had a best friend and I'd be honored to have her as mine.

A loud rumble of thunder made her jump a second before the heavens opened up and dumped a deluge of rain that was almost monsoonal.

"Oh my God, run for the car," she said, leaping to her feet and taking off at a sprint.

I didn't need any encouragement to follow but by the time we'd travelled the forty meters, we were soaked to the skin.

"There are blankets in the back seat. Get in," she said, all but shoving me into the back seat as she tumbled in behind me and slammed the door.

"I'm soaked." She looked down at her pale blue T-shirt and white Capris and shivered. "And cold."

I was too, but there was no way in hell I was going to make the obvious suggestion: that we get out of our clothes.

As if I'd telepathed my thoughts, her gaze locked onto mine as she slowly handed me a blanket. "We'll catch a chill if we drive back to Santa Monica like this."

She blushed. "We should take the wet things off and wrap up in the blankets."

I tsk-tsked. "You're always trying to get me naked."

I pointed at the sky, where sheets of rain continued to slice down. "I'm starting to think you'd go to extreme lengths, including plea to the big guy upstairs, to get my gear off."

She rolled her eyes. "You're onto me. I did a rain dance all afternoon just so I could see you strip again."

"You liked it well enough the first time." I shouldn't tease her but she looked so adorable, tendrils of hair clinging to her cheeks, her eyelashes spiked with water and rain drops trickling down her neck.

I dared not look lower because the sight of her wet T-shirt could just push me over the edge.

She tilted her nose in the air. "As I recall, the feeling was mutual."

To prove it, she peeled her T-shirt overhead before I could come up with one, sane reason why we shouldn't do this.

"Mia, we can't—"

"You want to risk pneumonia, fine, but don't tell me I can't do this." She unclipped her bra and slid it off, leaving me staring at her tits, pale and perfect.

I was grateful for the darkness and the secluded spot she'd chosen to park because damned if I wanted anyone else getting the chance to look at her.

"You're beautiful," I murmured, grabbing the nearest blanket to stop from grabbing her.

"Thanks." She unzipped her pants and struggled to push them down her legs, her thong tangling in the wet material.

I couldn't breathe. Couldn't speak. Couldn't do much of anything but gawk at this incredibly lovely woman. Wet and naked and wanting me.

After what seemed like an eternity, she draped a blanket around her shoulders and let it cover her body. But it was too late. The damage had been done.

I needed her with a ferocity that scared the crap out of me.

In the end, she took the decision out of my hands. She grabbed the hem of my polo shirt and slid it upward until it was off. When she reached for the zipper on my jeans, I stilled her hand. I'd been on edge all day with wanting her. If she touched my cock, I was in danger of regressing to my early teenage days and this would be over before it had begun.

My jeans and jocks came off in record time, but I had the foresight to grab the condom out of my wallet before the sodden mass hit the floor.

As Mia watched me with silent approval, I slid the condom on, then reached for her.

She straddled me, the blanket draping us in our own private cocoon.

Then she lowered herself on my cock and all I could think was how fucking right this felt.

I grabbed her arse in one hand and thumbed her clit with the other, pumping upward as she slid down, the friction between our bodies creating a welcome warmth beneath the blanket.

She arched back a little, thrusting her tits in my face, and I sucked one into my mouth, then the other, loving her pants and moans.

The pressure built in my balls, the promise of mind-numbing pleasure, as she rode me with an abandon that was incredible to watch.

I circled her clit faster as her breathing got shallower, waiting for her to fall off the edge before I followed in an orgasm that clamped my head in a vice as I shot my load.

I liked sex. Sex was fun. But sex with Mia? Fuck. Indescribable.

She sank into my arms and I cuddled her, wanting to shut out reality for a little while longer.

A reality that insisted we couldn't do this, no matter how badly I wanted to.

TWELVE
MIA

When I was a teenager and needed to blow off steam, I'd head to the Santa Monica Pier.

I loved the vibe. The hip people, the cosmopolitan feel, the chance to lose myself in a sea of humanity.

Tonight was different. I didn't need to blow off steam or blend in with the crowd. I was with Kye and what we'd done in the car two hours ago? Made me more relaxed than I'd been in ages.

"Want to see Pacific Park or the aquarium?" I snuck a glance at our joined hands, not caring what we did as long as I got to feel this good.

"I'm happy just strolling," he said, threading his fingers through mine. "It's a nice night for it."

"Even in damp clothes?" I grinned at the memory of the struggle we had getting back into our wet clothes. Hard enough getting dressed in a car.

He ducked his head to whisper in my ear. "With the heat you generate, babe, your clothes should be steaming."

Some of that heat found its way into my cheeks. "Right back at you."

Our gazes locked and my nerve endings zinged like they always did when he looked at me.

I wished I knew what he was thinking but while I was feeling this good, no way would I risk another lecture on why we couldn't be more than friends.

We were together, in this moment, and I intended on making the most of it before we headed back to the academy all too soon.

I blinked and the intimacy enveloping us dissipated. "This was my go-to place when I was a kid."

When he smiled, the corners of his eyes crinkled adorably. "Yeah? I wouldn't think a pampered princess like you would need to get away."

I rolled my eyes and bumped him with my hip. "Believe me, every teen girl needs to get away at some point."

"Let me guess. Your dad didn't buy you a pony?"

"More like he was never around, always on the road playing tournaments, and when he was here he tried to overcompensate."

Kye remained silent, his pity palpable.

"Don't feel sorry for me, because it wasn't that bad." In fact, I'd idolized my dad and hadn't begrudged him his career, despite not seeing him for a good chunk of every year. But being back home was making me maudlin. "I just didn't like him smothering me."

"It's natural he'd be overprotective." His gaze slid over me like warm treacle. "I mean, look at you."

"Thanks, but if I'm dorky now, I was worse back then."

He smiled. "Perm? Glasses? Braces?"

"Two out of three."

"Which ones?"

"Like I'd tell you." Having the hot guy trying to imagine

me with a perm and braces wasn't how I wanted to end tonight.

"I'll find out."

"Like hell." I bumped him with my hip again and he bumped back, the gesture soft and teasing and perfect for the way we were in sync tonight. "What about you? Did you have a mullet and wear acid washed jeans?"

"I'm not that old," he said, the previous warmth in his tone replaced by a deliberate coolness that saddened me.

We had a physical connection, a great one. But the sooner I figured out that didn't equate to anything more, the better off I'd be.

I shouldn't push him, should retreat back to banter. But I wanted to know more about Kye. Wanted to know everything.

Because while I could logically pass this off as a physical fling, emotionally I was already craving answers to so many questions.

"Or were you one of those tennis jocks, too cool for school?"

His lips compressed and his expression tightened, before he released a reluctant breath. "I was a loner. Learned it was easier to keep away from people than face the consequences."

From what he'd already told me about his mom, I could guess what he'd been through. "You were teased and got into a lot of fights?"

He nodded, his somberness making me want to hug him and make it all better. "Guys were jerks. Always making lewd comments about Mum. Trying to use me to get into the strip club underage." He gripped my hand so tight I wiggled my fingers and he immediately eased off the pressure. "Sorry."

"Don't be. I get how mad that stuff must've made you."

"You have no idea." His icy tone made me want to rub my bare arms.

Wishing I'd never started digging, I tried to alleviate the mood. "At the risk of sounding like an ignorant American cliché, was your go-to place the Sydney Opera House?"

The corners of his mouth twitched. "Is that the only Sydney landmark you know?"

I placed a hand over my heart. "Guilty as charged."

His eyes glazed over for a moment, as if he was deep in thought. "My go-to place was Rushcutters Bay. I liked the calm of the water after the hustle bustle of the Cross."

Glad he was finally opening up, I risked pushing him further. "What's the Cross like?"

"Chaotic. Sleazy. Dangerous."

A little shiver ran up my spine at his audible bleakness. "I grew up there, and Mum was known as a local, so I was usually safe."

He shook his head, his faraway gaze fixed on the end of the pier. "But I saw too many kids arrive at the Cross looking for adventure and a good time, kids who ended up druggies or hookers or dead."

A lump formed in my throat. "Was tennis your go-to place too?"

His head snapped up and he fixed me with a startled stare. "How the fuck do you know me so well when we barely know each other?"

"I-I ... care about you," I said, sounding lame but meaning it and terrified he'd clam up more now than he had before. "I think we click with some people in this world and time's irrelevant."

I expected him to scoff so when he took my other hand

and squeezed both before looking into my eyes, I melted a little.

"We click, huh?"

"Absolutely." I nodded, sounding way more emphatic than I felt.

Truth was, I wanted to click with Kye so badly I could taste it. The burning question was, did he want to click with me?

"I don't click with many people in this world," he said, dropping a light kiss on the tip of my nose. "But if I had to click with anyone, it'd be someone just like you."

I wanted to kiss him and hug him and not let go.

I settled for a goofy grin. "Want to grab a hot dog?"

"Nah, let's head back."

And just like that, my fantasy bubble burst.

Kye blew hot and cold. I knew that.

Why did I have to fall for a guy who'd shut me out as soon as he let me in?

THIRTEEN
KYE

I was in deep shit.

Worse than the time I'd been surrounded by a gang of bullies near the fountain at the Cross. Worse than the time I'd been busted by Mum peeping at the girls getting dressed when I was thirteen. Worse than the time Dad had been called to the Academy after I'd busted that dickhead's nose and he'd stared at me with disappointment and pity.

Yep, hanging with Mia, holding her hand, sharing snippets of our past, was way worse than any of those other times. Because this time, I didn't want to get away.

I wanted to do this forever, sharing hot dogs on Santa Monica Pier, pretending like we were just another couple. But we weren't. We couldn't be. Not when my future depended on staying away from her.

"We should head back." I slurped the last of my soda and lobbed it in the trash.

"Guess so." But she didn't move and I couldn't blame her.

It had been fun playing hooky for a few hours, like we didn't have a care in the world. When we both knew better.

"I'm going to talk to my dad," she said, so softly I had to lean closer to hear her. "Tell him about us."

"No." I leapt to my feet and tugged my hand free from her grip. "Are you insane?"

An elderly couple strolling nearby shot me a disapproving glare and I lowered my voice. "I'll be out on my arse as soon as he hears my name associated with yours."

I paced a few steps before turning back, dread curdling the orange soft drink in my gut. "Don't you get it? I'm on my last chance. Screw this up and I'm dead."

"Don't be so melodramatic." She stood and squared her shoulders, way too calm while I was freaking out. "We'll sort this out."

I shook my head. "No way. There's nothing to sort." I gestured between us. "You and me? We're nothing."

The moment the words slipped out I wished I could take them back. She looked stricken, like I'd slapped her.

I tried again. "What I mean is—"

"Didn't know you were a liar as well as a dipshit," she said, blinking rapidly.

Ah fuck, I'd made her cry too.

"What I meant to say was, we can't be anything to each other no matter how much we may want it." That sounded so lame.

She stopped blinking and pinned me with a wide-eyed stare that made me want to cuddle her all night long. "Does that mean you want it?"

"No ... yes ... fuck," I muttered, increasingly out of my depth.

I knew what I wanted. I just couldn't have her at the risk of my career and disappointing my dad yet again. He was a good guy. Who'd taken a chance on a loser like me. I owed him and this time, I'd pay up.

"I get it." She sounded so solemn and I wished we could revert to the happy, laughing couple we'd been an hour ago, cramming fairy floss and hot dogs into our mouths, joking around, carefree. "You're a chicken-shit as well as a liar."

There was nothing remotely funny about this situation but I found myself smiling anyway. Mia was a hell of a woman. Smart and funny and willing to fight for us.

She was right. I was a chicken-shit. But there were some things in life that couldn't be messed with and my future at the Cresswell Academy was one of them.

I had to make her understand and to do that, I'd need to give her a snippet of the truth.

"Was your dad around when you aced your first test? Your first ballet recital? Your graduation?"

She nodded, eyeing me with wariness.

"My dad wasn't. He didn't know I existed." I held out my hands, palms up, nothing to hide. "When Mum died and he turned up, I was resentful. He should've known about me. He should've been there for me."

I fist-pumped my chest. "But it wasn't his fault that Mum kept me a secret. And when it counted, he stepped up."

Inhaling a deep breath, I blew it out, buying time, hoping I could articulate half of what I was feeling without sounding like a dickhead. "He owed me nothing. But my dad made an effort to get to know me. He pulled strings for me. And even when I fucked up real bad, he still believed in me."

I hesitated, hating that a lump had welled in my throat. "Me, the loser kid who lived over a strip club his whole life, who hung out with pimps. He didn't care about any of that or how it could damage his reputation. He committed to me."

The burning in the back of my throat intensified but I'd be damned if I made a sissy of myself in front of a girl whose opinion mattered more than it should. "So think about all those times your dad was around for you, when he looked at you with pride."

I pressed my palms to my chest. "That's what I want. For my dad to look at me like he's proud of me. That I'm more than some screw-up he wished he still didn't know about."

A tear trickled down Mia's cheek, followed by another, and I bundled her into my arms before we were both bawling.

"Do you get it now?" I murmured into her hair, burying my nose in the soft fruity fragrance, imprinting it on my memory.

She didn't move for an eternity before I felt a gentle nod against my chest.

Good. I'd made her understand.

But at what cost?

FOURTEEN
MIA

Many people were intimidated by the great Dirk Cresswell.

Not me. My dad was a pushover if I played him right. Not that I deliberately set out to fool him but like any daughter knows, make the big eyes, make the lower lip wobble just a tad and throw in a healthy dose of admiration in that wide-eyed stare, and most dads would do anything for their little girls.

It had worked when I'd wanted to go camping with Dani at thirteen. It had worked when I'd wanted a convertible for my sixteenth. And it sure as hell better work now, when I needed to make my dad understand that Kye was a good guy, without tipping him off to how involved we already were.

Not that Kye saw it that way. Uh-uh, he'd made it clear in no uncertain terms just how 'over' we were last night. I understood his reticence. His declaration from the heart about seeking his dad's approval had made me cry.

But I didn't give up that easily.

I'd seen his reluctance to leave me when we'd made it back to the academy last night, had seen how torn he was.

He had feelings for me, no matter how much he wanted to deny it. And once he figured out my dad wasn't a big, bad ogre who'd kick him out on his ass if he found out about us, we could spend every spare moment together.

His tennis career was important to him, I got it. And I didn't want to mess that up for him. But what I felt when I was with him? Indefinable.

It wasn't just the sensational sex, which made me tingle just thinking about it. It was how he made me feel when I was with him: cherished, adored, and a little bit bad. When I was with Kye, I wasn't good girl Mia Cresswell, study nerd who achieved great grades but was lousy socially.

I was Mia, who made him smile and laugh and hold me tight.

I liked being just Mia. And I'd be damned if I sat back and did nothing, content to see Kye occasionally on the academy grounds but not much else.

I spied my dad exactly where I thought he'd be this early in the morning: at the practice courts, watching his protégés hit out. Perfect. He'd be in a good mood, as morning was his favorite part of the day.

"Guess who?" I covered his eyes with my hands, wondering if he'd remember the countless times I'd done this as a kid and how he'd deliberately make crazy guesses, each more outlandish than the last.

"Hmm, let me see ..." His hands covered mine, patting them. "Miley Cyrus? Lady GaGa? Katy Perry?"

I laughed. "If that's your attempt at trying to sound trendy, Dad, it sucks."

I lowered my hands and he spun around, embracing me in a bear hug that squeezed the air from my lungs.

"How are you, Chickadee?" He released me and I stared

at the man who'd raised me, the man who'd do anything for me, the only man in the world I truly trusted.

I was hoping to add Kye to that exclusive list.

"Fine, Dad. You?"

"Never better." He gestured at the grass courts. "Keeping these guys on their toes keeps me young."

I glanced at the court and tried to hide my surprise at seeing Kye smashing returns as fast as a machine served up balls. Guess I wasn't the only one who'd had a sleepless night and he'd come down here at the crack of dawn too.

"Looks like you've got some good prospects in this batch." I tried to sound casual and keep my gaze averted from Kye.

My dad wasn't a fool and the last thing I needed before I'd laid down the groundwork was to alert him to the fact I was crazy for Kye.

"Yeah, though time will tell." His eyes narrowed as he stared at Kye. "Not too sure about this one."

Uh hell.

"Kye?"

My dad's head swiveled toward me, his glare suspicious. "You know him?"

I made a split second decision to play it cool while delivering a semi-truth to test the waters. "Yeah, he seemed a little lost at your intro party the other night, so I showed him around LA yesterday."

"That's not like you, playing tour guide to the jocks." A frown appeared between my dad's brows. "You know you don't have to do that."

I shrugged. "I know, but I'm on vacation, and he seems nice, so I thought I'd do the right thing."

If my trite answer appeased my dad's suspicions, he didn't show it. "Be careful of Sheldon. He may appear nice on the surface but he's got a past and I'd prefer you kept your distance."

Uh-oh. This wasn't going to plan.

I'd wanted to ease into a conversation about Kye, pave the way to gaining Dad's approval. Instead, he'd warned me off? Shit.

"Dad, I'm not a little kid. I'm a pretty good judge of character and Kye seems—"

"What did you do yesterday?" Way too astute, my dad's steely gaze swung from me to Kye and back again, as I valiantly hoped he couldn't read my feelings for Kye on my face.

"Drove around and checked out the usual tourist spots in LA, then Santa Monica."

I willed the heat suffusing my body not to flush my cheeks in a dead giveaway that we'd done much more than drive around.

Sadly, I couldn't stop the blush and my dad's stare turned flinty. "Mia, you say you're a good judge of character but you know what guys on the circuit can be like."

His lips compressed, like he didn't want to say the rest. "These jocks have women throwing themselves at them all the time. They're transient, moving from one tournament to another."

He shook his head. "You're smarter than that."

I swallowed the anger tightening my throat. Dad didn't need to lecture me on tennis jocks. He'd been one of them and while he'd been continent hopping, I'd been home with a nanny, watching my dad on TV and pining for him.

As for his social life, I had to give him credit. He'd never brought any of his girlfriends home when I was young and I'd known there'd been plenty. I'd seen the photos online when I was eight. There were thousands of pictures and in the ones of him in a tux, he had a different beautiful woman on his arm.

I'd been jealous, that he would spend time with them and not me. Wasn't until I'd hit my teens and he retired did some of my resentment fade as I wondered why he'd never remarried. We'd spent a lot of time together when the academy became his permanent home and he wasn't flying off to tournaments all the time. I treasured those times.

Like how I treasured my time with Kye, no matter how limited I knew it to be.

"I am smart, Dad, which is why you should trust me."

Some of his anger faded as he swiped a hand over his face. "I do, baby, but I just don't want to see you get hurt."

"I won't." My gaze drifted to Kye, smashing those damn balls like his life depended on it. "Kye's determined to take his tennis to the next level and believes he can do that while training here. Your support would mean a lot."

If Dad perceived I was talking about more than tennis, he didn't let on.

"Just be careful," he said, slinging an arm over my shoulder as we both watched Kye.

As I leaned into Dad and rested my head on his chest, I wondered if I'd achieved my goal of easing him into the idea of Kye and me being together, or if I'd screwed up majorly and ended Kye's career for good.

FIFTEEN
KYE

I had a bad feeling about this.

My gut twisted with anxiety as Mia and Dirk watched me. What was she saying to him? If she mentioned our relationship, I was a dead man.

Not that we had a relationship, per se, but the fact I hadn't slept all night after deliberately blowing her off by revealing some of my innermost fears pretty much meant I wished we were involved.

But it was impossible. I had to stay focused. And every time I smashed a strong forehand or killer backhand down the line, albeit against a serving machine, took me one step closer to repaying my debt to Dad and getting what I'd craved since we'd first met: his approval.

My dad had said all the right things and done all the right things since he'd discovered I'd existed, but I suspected it was out of obligation rather than any great pride in having a son.

I often wondered if I'd deliberately fucked up by smashing that jerk's nose in Sydney to test Dad's commitment to me. Bizarre? Hell yeah, but the anger that bubbled up at times was fuelled by resentment: at losing Mum, at losing the only home I'd ever known, at losing my innocence way too young.

When most kids around me were heading to the skateboard ramp to swap footy cards, I was dodging syringes in back alleys and running errands for Mum's girls. Not that Mum knew. She would've killed me if she'd known the strippers were paying me pocket money to do odd jobs for them. Nothing illegal, thank God, but I'd seen enough of the seedy underworld as a kid to last a lifetime.

And that shit made me angry and resentful. Why did some kids get to have cushy lives and others didn't? Why did they have fathers who attended rugby games and school presentations, while I'd had to use my fists to fend off the insults aimed at Mum?

That despite doing her best to give us a good life, Mum had died anyway. Did I blame her for not telling Dad I'd been born? Shit yeah. But even if she had, would Australia's mega TV personality have wanted to know me?

Doubtful. Highly doubtful. Which made me question his motives at wanting to know me now even more. I couldn't fault him so far: he'd been supportive and understanding and had come through for me, even after I'd stuffed up and been kicked out of the academy.

But the disappointment I'd glimpsed when he'd looked at me that day? Like I'd told Mia, it's what drove me. Every single day.

I had to be a gun tennis player, the best Australia had seen, because I owed my dad. I had to repay his faith in me, even if I didn't deserve it.

When the machine shut off, I propped my racket against the net and collected all the balls, feeding them back into the machine. I'd have to go another round because no way in hell was I heading off this court while Mia still stood next to Dirk.

I couldn't look at her without remembering how she felt in my arms, the soft panting sounds she made when I was inside her, the feel of her tongue against mine.

Fuck. Not helping. I turned away and envisioned icebergs.

By the time I was ready to go again, Mia had left and Dirk was striding across the court toward me.

"Your down the line forehand needs refining," he said, handing me my racket. "But your backhand is looking strong."

"Thanks." I took the racket, wondering if I'd ever lose the sense of awe I felt in his presence.

Dirk Cresswell was tennis royalty. Fifteen Grand Slams. Held the record for the fastest serve in the world. Churning out world-class winners from his academy here with ongoing regularity.

I was lucky to be here. I knew that. He knew that.

What he didn't know was how close I'd come to throwing it all away by sleeping with his daughter.

I hoped.

"Heard you hung out with Mia yesterday?"

I was so fucked.

Using the poker face I'd honed through years of facing insults about my Mum at school, I nodded. "Yeah. She was kind enough to play tour guide."

"Mia's got a good heart." He stared off into the distance and I was grateful to escape that penetrating stare. "I'd hate to see anyone take advantage of that."

Shit. Was he warning me off because he suspected or he knew what we'd done?

"Mia's aware my focus is on improving my tennis while

I'm here. I enjoyed our tour. But no one's taking advantage of anyone." I kept my tone light, devoid of emotion, desperate to get back to smashing balls and avoid any potential slip-ups.

Because unless Dirk was lulling me into a false sense of security before booting me out, he knew nothing and was just giving me the trite warning any father would give a guy like me.

"Glad to hear it." Dirk turned his head to stare at me and I felt the chill right down to my bones. "Because the thing is, Kye, I don't care how goddamn talented you are. And I don't give a rat's ass about your dad's friendship."

He took a step closer, trying to intimidate. "If you mess with my daughter in any way, I'll personally kick your ass back to Sydney so quick your head will spin faster than my world record serve you seem so determined to beat."

With that, he turned and strode away, and I exhaled the breath I'd been inadvertently holding.

On the upside, he seemed to think I had talent.

On the downside, he'd confirmed what I already knew. Screw with Mia and I was out on my ass.

What if it were too late?

SIXTEEN
KYE

Fourteen days into executing my grand plan of pushing Mia away, I wondered what the hell I was doing.

During the first week, I'd lost every single one of my practice matches in a major trial and been the laughing stock of my fellow trainees. In the second week, I'd lost my temper on court when a younger opponent had whipped the pants off me. And when I wasn't serving double faults or missing lobs, I was touchy, grouchy and thoroughly pissed off.

Not to mention the worst case of blue balls I'd ever had.

Wasn't like I'd had a ton of sex, despite what dickheads at school used to say because of where I lived and my access to strippers. But looked like having sex with Mia made me crave more, with her, in a big way and it was seriously putting me off my game.

To make matters worse, I'd deliberately snubbed her. Several times. Once when she'd waited for me after an in-house tournament, another when she'd ambushed me outside my villa.

I wasn't proud of the way I'd treated her both times—

cold, aloof, almost cruelly cutting—but it was the only way to keep my sanity and keep my deal with myself, and Dad, unofficially.

Dirk's warning a fortnight ago only cemented what I already knew. Any involvement with Mia would spell the end of my stint here, and the end of my burgeoning tennis career.

The stupid thing? I wouldn't mind so much if it were only me involved, but the prospect of facing Dad's disappointment again? No way in hell I'd let that happen.

"Your game today sucked."

I glanced up from my squatting position where I was packing my bag, to see Mia standing over me, hands on hips, looking like an avenging angel in a mid-thigh white summer dress that made me want to drag her down to lose the halo.

"Tell me something I don't know," I muttered, zipping the bag and straightening. "I've got a post-match meeting with one of the coaches so I'll see you round—"

"You're avoiding me. I get it." She pinned me with a no-nonsense stare that alerted me to the fact this wouldn't be an easy brush-off like the other times. "Didn't pick you for a coward."

I glanced around, not wanting to have this conversation with witnesses. Everyone else had left, leaving me no excuse to bolt. "We've been through this, Mia. You know why we can't—"

"What? Why we can't be friends?" She wrinkled her nose. "Shit, Kye, I get why we can't be involved. You spelled it out pretty fucking clearly that night on the pier. But I thought ..."

My heart fissured a little at the bleakness in her beautiful brown eyes. "What?"

She took a deep breath before blurting out, "I thought we had something beyond sex."

I wanted to say 'we did'. I wanted to say a lot of things. But none of them would make this any easier on either of us.

"You said fuck. Wow, you've been misinterpreting our time together a lot," I said, sounding deliberately flippant, and I saw the exact moment the sadness in her eyes morphed to anger.

"Want to hear it again?" She leaned in close and I braced against the relentless urge to haul her into my arms and bury my nose in her divine smelling hair. "Fuck you, Kye. I hope your self-delusions keep you warm at night."

With that, she stalked away, all long, tanned legs and indignation.

I wanted to run after her.

I wanted to tell her everything.

Instead, with my heart as leaden as my legs, I picked up my bag, hoisted it over my shoulder, and waited until she'd disappeared into the clubhouse before heading for the showers.

SEVENTEEN

MIA

"So what's with you and the boy from Oz?" Dani gestured toward the clubhouse bar where a group of jocks were gathered. "Summer fling over?"

"Something like that." I took a swig from my beer, my gaze fixed on Kye.

If looks could kill, he'd be six feet under.

"Pity," Dani said, downing half her Margarita in a gulp. "He's hot."

Didn't I know it.

I also knew that Kye Sheldon was an arrogant, lying prick.

He thought I was an idiot who'd buy into his whole push-me-away act. Dumbass. But I was done trying to approach him. He'd made sure of that yesterday with his deliberate snide-ness.

Too bad for him I didn't give up easily. And I could play childish games just as well as he could.

"You like him." Dani's eyes narrowed as her curious gaze flicked between the two of us. "Really like him."

"Maybe." My noncommittal response hid a world of

hurt. Because I more than 'liked' Kye. Which was totally crazy, because we barely knew each other and hadn't spent a lot of time together, but there was something about him that made me feel ... special.

"He's playing hard to get, huh?"

I nodded. "It's complicated, him being at the academy and Dad's overprotectiveness."

Dani's brow crinkled. "That hasn't stopped your dad foisting you off on those boring tennis jocks in the past."

"That's because he could control those guys ..." It came to me in a flash, why I really liked Kye.

I liked his underlying hint of wildness, his nonconformity, his confidence in himself to go it alone.

He possessed all those admirable qualities I didn't.

I was drawn to him because of it and it only served to intensify my feelings.

He'd accused me of slumming it at the start, of taking a walk on the wild side for a night. That may have been true but now that I'd been on the wild side, I wanted more. I craved it. And I hated being denied.

"By the looks of your bad boy Aussie, no-way no-how Dirk could control him." Dani popped a peanut into her mouth, chewed, then smirked. "Bet the Aussie got warned off you by Daddy Dearest."

I'd wondered the same thing myself after my chat with Dad. He'd know the power he held over Kye's future and if it came to protecting me, I was damn sure Dad would use it.

"Doesn't mean Kye had to listen," I muttered, draining the rest of my beer before slamming the bottle on the table.

"No balls," Dani said, pushing the peanut dish toward me.

I shook my head and nudged it back. "He has them, and they're magnificent."

Dani let out a whoop that had several of the guys at the bar glancing our way. Except Kye. He deliberately turned his back on me.

"Brrr ... chilly." Dani rubbed her upper arms and pretended to shiver. "Hey, I know how we can have some fun."

If Dani suggested visiting the local male revue club again, I'd pass. The only naked male body I wanted to see was Kye's.

"How?"

She leaned across the table and cupped her hands before whispering, "Make the Aussie jealous."

"Uh-uh." I shook my head, not wanting to go down that route. I didn't want to give some other guy the wrong idea and lead him on, and despite how much Kye's cold behavior had hurt me, I didn't want to hurt him.

Dani snapped her fingers under my nose. "Wake up, sweetie. The Aussie is a tennis jock, which means he's driven by testosterone like the rest of his Neanderthal species. He understands competition. He thrives on it and is driven to win."

Dani sat back, smug. "What if you were the prize?"

Okay, when Dani put it like that, a small part of me couldn't help but agree. Nothing else I'd said or done had made an impact with Kye. I'd watched him at warm-ups, I'd turned up at his practice games, and I'd tried confronting him. Nada success on all counts.

What if making him jealous was the one thing to snap him out of his self-imposed no-go zone?

"So you think I should flirt with one of those deadheads?" I pointed at the bar and Dani's eyes lit up.

"Abso-frikking-lutely." She rubbed her hands together. "Now, let's see. Who'd be best to make the Aussie green?"

I scanned the guys, not feeling the remotest buzz despite a few of them being really cute. They all had great bodies; that was a given considering how hard they worked out at the academy. And some of them had nice smiles. But none came close to giving me the electrifying zap I felt when I looked at Kye.

"How about him?" Dani pointed to the tall guy at the end of the bar nearest Kye. "Cute ass in denim. Broad pecs. Well defined biceps. Prominent bulge—"

"Okay, he'll do," I said, cutting off what could be one of Dani's detailed fantasized accounts of how the proportion of the bulge equaled screaming orgasms. "Wish me luck."

I stood, grateful when the waiter deposited another round of drinks at our table at that moment, providing me with an extra dose of liquid courage. I downed my beer as fast as I could gulp, savoring the head rush and hoping it would last.

"Go get him, girlfriend," Dani said, grinning as I slipped off my watch and slid it into my bag before making a beeline for the bar.

As if sensing my approach, Kye's shoulders stiffened and he didn't turn around.

I'd soon remedy that.

Insinuating my way between Tall Guy and a baby-faced guy I recognized as Kye's practice partner, I subtly bumped arms with my intended. "Excuse me. Do you have the time?"

Tall Guy stopped talking with Baby Face and glanced at me, initial irritation giving way to interest when he saw me. "Sure, Mia, but only if you agree to have a drink with me."

"Deal." I nodded, flashing what I hoped was my best flirtatious smile as I heard a subdued growl from Kye over Tall Guy's shoulder.

Good. I'd captured his attention. Time to ramp it up. "By the way, I don't know your name?"

I laid a hand on Tall Guy's arm and resisted batting my eyelashes, just.

"Pete." His grin was too predatory for my liking and I removed my hand. "Though I would've hoped you wouldn't have to ask, what with my heading the leader board of the in-house tournaments."

Ugh. He had an ego to match his height.

"I don't get to all the games, but I'll be sure to try and make more of yours," I said, laying it on thick.

"I'll look out for you." The way his stare roved my body, I just bet he would. "What would you like to drink?"

There was a difference between alcohol-fuelled courage and fuzzy brain syndrome that might make me do something stupid, so I settled for a safe option.

"Lime and soda, please." I added a fake giggle to convince Pete I needed a soda and not more alcohol.

His eyebrows rose. "Hey, we're the ones forced to abstain." He leaned in close, too close, and my skin prickled with distaste. "Why don't you indulge? Go wild?"

I would. With Kye. Who had turned at the sound of my stupid fake laugh and was now staring at me with concern.

I should've been happy I'd captured his attention, but all I felt was anger. A deep-seated fury that he'd left me no choice but to resort to childish games to get his attention, when all I wanted was to have some one-on-one time with him, chatting and laughing and having fun, like we did in LA.

"What the hell, make it a vodka, lime and soda." With

Kye looking on, I gazed up at Pete adoringly, while pressing my arm against his. "I'm all for going wild."

I was over the top with the flirting, but seeing Kye watching me with disapproval pushed all my buttons.

I wanted to rile him, to make him do *something*.

What I didn't want was him walking out.

But that's exactly what he did.

EIGHTEEN
KYE

When the blackness descended, I had to escape.

In the past, when I'd felt it creep up on me, I'd do whatever it took to work it off. Which usually meant holding it in until I reached the courts. That was the great thing about smacking around a tennis ball. It couldn't smack you back.

I'd learned that lesson in fourth grade. And fifth. And sixth. Black eyes and cracked cheekbones and broken noses weren't so good when I was on the receiving end. So I'd wised up. Picked up a tennis racket. And never looked back.

But how I was feeling right now, I couldn't risk heading to the courts in case someone saw me or worse, approached me. I needed to be alone. Some place I could work it off without letting loose on anyone.

The pool.

Tucked away in the back corner of the property, it would be the perfect place to blow off steam in seclusion. It took me five minutes to reach it, another minute to pick the lock and let myself in, and thirty seconds to strip down to my boxers and dive in.

The second I submerged I felt some of the tension

ease. Yeah, this would help dissipate the blackness that threatened to consume me when I saw Mia pressing against Pete.

I hadn't expected to feel anything, let alone the all-consuming jealousy that made me want to drag Pete away from the bar and beat him to a pulp.

It should've been okay, seeing Mia flirt with him. It's what I wanted, for her to leave me alone. But seeing her smile at that dufus, and giggle, and talk about going wild ... Fuck, I sluiced through the water like a madman was on my tail at the thought of her doing anything with Pete, let alone going wild.

I lost count of how many laps I swam. I didn't care, as long as the blackness receded, worked out of my system by repetitive exercise before I did something monumentally stupid: like head back to the bar and ensure Pete couldn't leave with Mia if both his legs were broken.

When my muscles screamed with fatigue, I stopped and rolled onto my back, floating in what was finally a sea of calm.

Until I heard a splash and opened my eyes to see Mia less than two feet away. In her underwear.

∽

MIA

I KNOW what prompted me to strip down to my underwear and hop into the pool with Kye.

The sheer, unadulterated urge to drown him.

I wanted to duck his head under the water and hold it there until he saw sense. Instead, all I succeeded in doing was startling him enough to have him go under for a few seconds before he bobbed up, coughing and spluttering and looking mad as hell.

"What the fuck are you doing?"

"Same thing as you." I smirked, knowing it'd annoy him. "Taking a midnight dip."

"Go away." He shook his head, water droplets spraying. "You can't be here right now."

"I can be anywhere I goddamn like." I folded my arms, belatedly realizing the affect it would have when his gaze riveted to my chest. And secretly pleased when I glimpsed the instant flare of heat in his eyes. "And for the record? You're done telling me what I can and can't do."

I half expected him to haul himself out of the water and leave without looking back. Instead, he took a step closer, causing ripples to lap at my waist.

"While I've given you no reason to trust me, I need you to listen when I say I really need to be alone right now."

His grim tone scattered goosebumps across my skin and for the first time since I'd dived in, I questioned the logic of my impulsive action in following him here.

"Why? What are you going to do? Dunk me—"

His mouth slammed on mine, stealing my breath, stealing my sanity, stealing my heart.

I couldn't breathe as he devoured my mouth and I let him, making embarrassing moaning sounds that echoed down to my soul.

He didn't let up the pressure as he backed me against the side of the pool, his pelvis grinding against mine, making me wish our underwear would disappear.

I knew Kye wasn't a guy to be pushed. Hell, his whole demeanor at times scared me. He was too intense, too closed off. But I'd fallen for him faster than was good for either one of us and I wanted him, for however long I could have him.

He palmed my breasts, sending slivers of heat shooting lower where I yearned for him to touch me. I grabbed his ass, pulled him tighter against me if that were possible. And all the while his tongue worked magic on mine, his long, hot, open-mouthed kisses making me melt. I was weightless, floating, and it had nothing to do with the buoyancy of the water.

I knew he was kissing me to prove a point, out of retribution for defying him. I didn't care. Because this crazy, unstoppable passion between us? I would never get enough.

All too soon he wrenched his mouth from mine. "You shouldn't be here," he said, sounding tortured.

"So you keep saying." I looped my arms around his neck. "But I'm not going anywhere."

He stared at me, admiration warring with anger in his expressive blue eyes. "Why are you doing this?"

A simple enough question, one I had no hope of answering. At least, not with the truth.

So I settled for a response as close to total honesty as I could get. "Because when we're together, you make me feel good. Happy. In a way I've never been."

He blinked. Once. Twice. But not before I'd glimpsed a tenderness that made my throat clog with unshed tears.

"You're not going to give up, are you?"

I shook my head, relieved his tone had lost the underlying chill and he sounded more resigned than anything else.

"I'm not worth it," he said so softly I barely heard him. "Please, just leave me alone."

His words may have been harsh but his body didn't lie, and for a guy who was doing his best to push me away, his hands spanned my waist and held on tight, like he never wanted to let me go.

I shook my head. "I can't."

Cupping his face between my hands, I looked him straight in the eye. "You are so worth it. Please come back to my villa. Stay with me tonight."

I knew I shouldn't have asked him. He could lose everything.

But I'd never let that happen. I'd threaten to disown my dad if he ever booted Kye out for being with me. And if there's one thing I was sure of, it was my dad's love.

He'd do anything for me. And if it came down to a choice between punishing Kye and pleasing me, I was pretty sure he'd choose the latter.

It made me feel like a heartless bitch, toying with Kye's future like this. I had nothing to lose in our relationship; he had everything. But I'd fight for him, would defend him, if it ever came to a showdown between the two men in my life.

"Please don't say no." I guided his head lower and kissed him, a soft glide of my lips against his that made me yearn for so much more. "I need you."

He resisted for a few seconds, before leaning his forehead against mine and I knew I had him.

"Okay."

One, simple word, laden with so much promise.

NINETEEN
MIA

With some people, no words were needed. I had a study partner at college like that, Maggie, a girl I could sit with for hours and we only talked if we needed to. I liked that about her, her economy with words.

It was like that with Kye. When we got back to my villa, we didn't speak. Didn't need to. We peeled off our clothes, stepped into the shower and washed each other.

I soaped his back, his front, lower. He returned the favor until I was mindless and boneless and desperate to have him inside me.

He toweled us off, carried me to the bed, and lay me down on top of the covers, his gaze scorching every inch of my bare skin as he studied me from top to bottom.

I opened my arms to him and he made fast work of a condom before lowering himself on top of me. Raining kisses on my collarbone. My neck. My breasts.

He sucked a nipple into his mouth as he entered me, inch by exquisite inch, taking his sweet time, knowing it drove me crazy.

I arched upward when he reached the hilt, the fullness

of him inside me almost too perfect, and it actually brought tears to my eyes. He kissed them away, not freaked like I expected him to be. Instead, his gaze locked on mine, steady and soft, as he slid in and out, setting a delicious rhythm that made me wish we could do this forever.

I had no idea how long we made love. Five minutes. Fifty. But all too soon the pleasure escalated and peaked, catapulting us to a place where lovers like us actually had a chance at forever.

When Kye pulled the covers over us, and I lay snuggled against his side, only then did he speak.

"You need to know about the blackness."

Not quite the opening line I'd expected after the incredible union we'd just shared, but this was momentous. Kye wanting to share anything with me was a bonus.

I rolled onto my side and rested my hand on his chest, directly over his heart. "Tell me."

He didn't glance at me, his gaze fixed firmly on the ceiling. "It started when I was in my early teens and the boys at school ramped up their teasing. They said horrible things about Mum. About me. About the girls who worked at the club."

I felt him tense beneath my palm.

"Most of the women who stripped were single mothers supporting their kids, or girls trying to pay their way through uni. They didn't want that lifestyle but did whatever it took to make ends meet."

I remained silent, waited for him to continue.

"Those jerks at my school were so judgmental and I mostly handled their crap. But then the blackness would creep over me at times."

Did he mean depression? Or anger?

"I hated it. Made me feel helpless. I didn't want to be a

victim to my rage and I sure as hell didn't want to hurt anyone, so I walked away time and time again. Wagged school when it got bad. Eventually picked up a tennis racket and figured hitting a ball hard was better than taking my frustrations out on some dickhead's nose."

"Is that how you started playing tennis?"

He nodded. "Yeah, at thirteen. Coaches couldn't believe I was a late starter. They marveled at my forehand." He snorted. "They didn't know I was imagining every prick's face who'd ever insulted Mum on those balls as I hammered them down the line."

"Sounds like good motivation."

"Tennis became my lifeline. Kept me sane even in the darkest times, like when Mum died."

My heart swelled with pity. How hard it must've been for this incredible guy to face insults and worse, the death of a parent alone.

While I'd always wished for a mom, especially those picture-perfect ones some of the girls had—the cookie-baker-lemonade-makers—and I'd loved hanging around Dani's outrageously flamboyant mom, I couldn't miss what I'd never had.

Mom had died when I was a toddler and I couldn't remember a thing about her. Sure, Dad showed me pics but it wasn't the same as having flesh and blood memories. Like what Kye had obviously treasured and lost.

"It must've been awful, losing your only parent." My arm slid across his chest and squeezed him tight.

"Mum was the best."

In those four, whispered words, I heard a wealth of subdued pain and sorrow.

"She inherited the club from some older guy she'd dated. He owned a bunch of businesses all over Sydney and thought Mum was the only woman he knew with big enough balls to run a strip club in the Cross and not care about the inevitable crap that would fly her way."

He sounded a million miles away, lost in his memories. Memories he now trusted me with. It was a huge step in our relationship.

"Apparently Dad came into the club one night on a buck's night. Love at first sight. They hooked up for a few months, then Dad was offered a role in a B grade flick in LA." His voice tightened with emotion. "Mum knew she was pregnant by then but didn't tell him because acting was his dream and she didn't want to wreck that for him."

"Wow, your mom sounds amazing."

He nodded. "She was. So they broke up and Dad left for LA. But his big break fell through. He stayed in LA for a year, trying to break into the Hollywood scene with little success. Headed back to Australia, got offered a talk show hosting gig and never looked back."

I wondered if asking a question would stop the flow of his revelations, but curiosity egged me on. "And your mom didn't tell him you'd been born once he returned, even though his career in LA never took off?"

"She didn't want to drag him down and damage his reputation as his career took off." He sounded pissed. "She was so damn self-sacrificing."

I didn't blame him for being angry. If his mom had told the truth, Kye would've had a father all those years he'd missed out.

"So how did he show up after your mom died?"

Some of the tension bunching his muscles beneath my palm eased. "Mum organized everything with a lawyer in case she died. Included a letter with a copy of the birth certificate, where she'd named him as the father. And a sample of my hair if he wanted to run a paternity test. He did. Turned up on our doorstep the day after she died."

I squeezed him tight again. "I'm so sorry."

He continued as if he hadn't heard me. "Dad was pretty amazing. Didn't try to muscle in but helped me with whatever I wanted done. Stood by me through the funeral. Organized the sale of the club. Invested the money for me." He swallowed. "And he's been looking out for me ever since."

Tears burned the back of my eyes. "Not wanting to disappoint him is a powerful motivator for keeping away from me."

"Yeah, that's what I was trying to make you understand." He scooted a little away, only to roll onto his side to face me, his earnestness scaring me. "But tonight, when the blackness rolled over me as I watched you with that dickhead, I realized something."

"What?" I held my breath, hoping this would be the major turning point in our relationship.

He cupped my cheek, his thumb brushing my lower lip in a slow sweep that almost had me blubbering. "I figured I've spent my whole life worried about what other people think of me and reacting to their opinions. The anger that scares the crap out of me is a byproduct of that." A wry smile twisted his mouth. "At least, that's what the shrink I saw a few times after Mum died told me."

His hand drifted from my face to rest on my shoulder, strong, reassuring. "I don't want to disappoint my dad, nothing's changed there. But you're the best thing that's happened to me in years and I'd be a fool not to want to fight for you."

My heart soared as he huffed out a breath. "Your dad warned me off you. And the last thing I want to do is piss him off. And I sure as hell don't want to treat you like a dirty, little secret but if you want this?" He tapped his chest. "If you want us to work while you're on vacation? I'm willing to give it a go on the condition you don't tell anyone."

I opened my mouth to respond and he mock zipped his lips. "That means anyone, even your bestie Dani, okay?"

I'd offloaded my secrets on Dani for years when we'd been growing up, but if it meant losing what I'd just gained with Kye? No way in hell I'd tell her a thing.

"Deal." I held out my hand to shake on it and he laughed, a purely joyous sound that had me joining in, before he rolled me onto my back, grabbed my wrists and held them overhead, and pinned me with his body.

"I can think of better ways to celebrate our new arrangement," he murmured, lowering his head to nuzzle my neck, sending heat spiraling through my body. "Much better ways."

I couldn't agree more.

TWENTY

KYE

I was on fire.

Returning serves like a man possessed. Slamming consistent down-the-line winners. Serving ace after ace. Delivering backhand returns that had the small crowd watching the first inter-tournament oohing.

And I had no idea what the fuck was going on.

When I played tennis, especially big matches, I channeled my anger. Focused it. Used it. It had become a familiar friend over the years, one that never let me down.

Not today. Today I was a guy floating across the court playing like an automaton after an incredible night in Mia's arms.

Who knew I didn't have to be angry to play well?

And that was another thing. Telling Mia the truth, unburdening myself about my past, made me feel lighter than I had in years. I'd never told another living soul all that stuff, not the shrink I'd briefly seen after Mum died, not even the sports psychologist at the academy. Hell, I didn't trust anyone—apart from Dad, and even with him I was still wary—enough to reveal my feelings like that.

But having Mia come after me, having her fight for something she wanted when I was too chicken-shit to do it, made me realize I could spend a lifetime pushing away the good and embracing the bad. I could continue to be resentful of everything and everyone, or I could have a real crack at living.

Living outside of tennis, which I was fast recognizing as my emotional crutch.

When things pissed me off, I headed for the court.

When I was swamped by the anger, I headed for the court.

When I couldn't deal, I headed for the court.

I could become a bigger, better version of myself when I was on the court.

And as I bounced on the balls of my feet on the baseline, waiting for my opponent to serve in what I hoped would be the final game, I hoped today was a turning point. That when I won this match, it would prove—to me—that I could channel positivity rather than anger to drive me to be the best.

As my opponent tucked a spare ball into his short's pocket, I risked a quick glance at the bleachers, where Mia sat next to Dani. Even at this distance, she glowed. Luminous. Making me want to wrap this up ASAP and find a place we could celebrate in private.

But with her dad on the sidelines, ready to give every academy player an evaluation at the conclusion of this tournament, I knew that would be out of the question until tonight.

Date night.

We'd planned it in the wee small hours of the morning, after we'd had sex three times, each more stupendous than the last. Looked like unburdening my soul had given my libido a kick in the arse too. Not that I'd ever had a problem in that department, especially with Mia. She was hot. Incredibly so and I wrenched my gaze away from her before I distracted my opponent with more than a killer return.

The next four points flew by. The guy from a top club in Orange County double-faulted twice, missed a lob and couldn't return a forehand winner that zipped past him at a speed that surprised both of us.

As I shook hands with my opponent, who stared at me through narrowed eyes, I resisted the urge to peek in Mia's direction again. This was another thing that was new: needing the approval of a woman to feel validated.

Mum had always been my biggest supporter in everything I did, and while it meant a lot it kinda didn't count when my loudest, proudest cheerleader was related. But having Mia's support meant a lot. And that's what she'd been since we first met: supportive.

Despite how I'd treated her, the many different ways in which I'd tried to push her away, she'd persisted. She hadn't given up on me, even when I was feeling pretty shitty after I'd first arrived and almost given up on myself.

"Good game, kid." Dirk approached as I reached the sidelines. "Real good."

"Thanks." I wiped the handle of my racket with a towel before sliding it into its cover. "Are we doing an analysis now or do I have time to shower?"

"Go grab a shower and we'll save yours 'til last."

"No worries." However, as I picked up my bag and Dirk hadn't budged, I braced. He hadn't spoken to me much since warning me off Mia, unless it was to criticize or instruct while I was on the practice courts. So the fact he was hanging around now? Made me suspicious.

"What's changed, Sheldon?"

Uh-oh. "What do you mean?"

Dirk jerked his head at the court. "The way you played out there today? A far cry from your shitty intra-academy hit-out. And I like to figure out what motivates my players so we can hone it, use it and repeat it."

I deliberately schooled my expression into an impassive mask. No way no how would Dirk want to know what had motivated me today, or how much I wanted to repeat it.

"Guess I'm settling in."

"And improving your attitude." Dirk tilted his head, studying me. "I liked what I saw out there today. A lot. Keep playing like that and you're destined for great things."

Before I could respond, he held up his finger. "And just so you know? I don't dish out praise lightly." He slapped me on the back. "Keep up the good work, kid, and you'll go places."

Guilt pierced my glow from his praise. I was deceiving this man, going directly against his wishes. If he ever found out, I'd be out on my arse, killer game or not. But the only place I wanted to be right now was in Mia's arms so I'd continue to play it cool.

"Thanks. Appreciate you saying it." I hoisted my bag onto my shoulder. "See you later."

Another backslap and Dirk headed towards the clubhouse, where he'd start dissecting the games of every player. First time he'd done it I'd been appalled, especially as my intra-academy tournament had been a rout. The guys had given me shit for it too, making jibes like kangaroos couldn't hold a racket and I should stick to Australia's national sports, cricket or Aussie Rules.

It had bothered me at the time, having an icon of the game like Dirk pick apart my match and highlight every weakness. I wasn't a technical player. I didn't study the mechanics of shots, I just channeled my anger and hit the ball. Would be interesting to hear what he had to say today, considering every shot had felt like I was caressing the ball rather than slamming the crap out of it.

"Nice job, Sheldon." Pete loped toward me and I inadvertently stiffened. Just because I'd worked things out with Mia didn't mean I'd lost the urge to pummel the guy for coming onto her. "You can actually play."

I grunted a response and pushed past him, not expecting his hand to clamp on my bicep.

"Wait up."

When I glared at his hand, he got the message and released me. "What do you want?"

"A favor."

I didn't like his smarmy tone. "I don't do favors."

"Trust me. You'll like this one." He gestured at the stands where Mia and Dani were deep in conversation. "I need a wingman. Someone to entertain the slut in the micro mini while I have a real crack at Mia."

He elbowed me. "Double date. What do you say? Be a pal and give a guy a chance at sticking it to a fine piece of ass like Mia."

I saw red. Or black. Every fucking color under the rainbow as rage so strong I could taste it swamped me.

Not that I hadn't heard guys talk like this before. Hell, put a bunch of testosterone fuelled dickheads together in any sporting club and the trash talk was often punctuated with crap like what I'd just heard.

But this time was different. He was talking about the girl I l—liked.

I clenched and unclenched my hands several times, trying to release the fury tightening every muscle in my body, making me want to spring on Pete and pound him to a pulp.

When I didn't respond, Pete groaned. "Don't tell me you're a pillow-biter."

The fact he spoke as derogatorily about gays as he did women made me hate this prick all the more.

I needed to get away before I did something regrettable in front of the entire team. "But doesn't Dirk come down hard on any guy who goes near his daughter?"

"My dad played the circuit with Dirk so he'll be cool." Pete grinned and my skin crawled. "I've been wanting to nail Mia for years."

I walked away. That, or stuff up my last chance at the academy, and before I'd had a chance to spend quality time with Mia.

"You're a soft-cock, Sheldon."

I ignored Pete's taunt and kept walking. Before I ensured that Pete the Prick had no cock at all.

TWENTY-ONE
MIA

Kye had asked me out on a date.

A real, honest to goodness date: dinner, movie and a moonlit walk.

"Let's skip the movie," I said, bumping him with my hip. "I'd rather spend the next few hours talking with you than keeping my mouth shut."

"Who said it would be?" He stopped where Santa Monica Beach gave way to Venice Beach, and tugged me closer. "Movies can be fun. We could make out for the entire time?"

I laughed. "We can do that and more back at my villa."

"Later." He ducked his head to nip my earlobe and I squealed. "You're insatiable."

"Only for you." I pressed my lips against his, loving the feel of his arms wrapped around my waist.

When we broke apart, a small frown creased his brow. "Pete's going to ask you out."

I shrugged. "So? He's probably been doing that to anything in a skirt for years."

"He's a lowlife."

"Tell me something I don't know." I winced. "That wasn't my finest moment, using him to make you jealous."

"You got that right." He whacked me playfully on the arm. "You could've just tried talking to me."

I rolled my eyes. "I did and you didn't want to listen, remember? And you kept pushing me away." I made a chattering motion with my hand. "Constantly saying stuff like you weren't good for me. Blah, blah, blah."

He captured my hand, raised it to his lips and brushed a kiss across the back of it, a strangely old-fashioned gesture that made me swoon. "I'm not good enough for you. Not by a long shot. But for some unfathomable reason, you bring out the best in me and I like feeling this good."

Not the most eloquent declaration but I liked how he couched things in his own way, spoken directly from the heart.

A tad overwhelmed by the feelings he elicited, I aimed for levity. "Come back to my villa and I guarantee to make you feel real good."

"Stop. Date night now. Down and dirty later." He tweaked my nose and I marveled at how far we'd come.

"Okay, Romeo, what's next?"

"Fairy floss," he said, with an emphatic nod.

"You mean cotton candy?"

"Semantics. Spun sugar tastes the same regardless of name."

"Aussie."

"Yank."

"Hot."

"Hotter." He pressed himself against me to prove it. "You're by far the hottest woman I've ever met."

I snorted, secretly thrilled he found me attractive. "Considering you hang out with tennis jocks twenty-four-seven, that's faint praise."

He slid his arms around my waist and I love how we fit together. "What do you want me to say? That your eyes remind me of melted chocolate mixed with caramel? That your skin glows like you're lit from within? That your hair is like silk?"

He laughed as my eyes narrowed. "Many of the girls who worked at the club read romance novels in their spare time. I'd hear them quote stuff like that."

"And you remembered it?" I patted his cheek. "Here I was, thinking you're a macho Aussie when you're actually a marshmallow."

"Soft center. Hard everywhere else." He pressed his pelvis against me to prove it. "On second thoughts, let's skip the fairy floss and head back to your villa."

I'd love nothing better but if this was to be one of few dates we shared, I wanted to make the most of it.

"Want to hear something corny?" I rested my palms on his chest. "I don't date much and I really want to make this one last."

Understanding sparked in those incredible blue eyes I could lose myself in forever. "Ditto."

Probably not the best time to ask, but curiosity had been eating away at me. "You don't do relationships?"

He made a cute little scoffing sound. "You're kidding? Girls at high school didn't come near me because their parents would kill them for hanging around a kid from a strip club. And later at the academy, the focus was tennis, not dating."

A faint pink stained his cheeks as he glanced over my

shoulder, before meeting my gaze again. "You're a first for me."

His honesty warmed me. "How so?"

"I've dated casually over the years. Had quite a few one night stands." His eyes softened. "But the way we've hung out? How we've talked?" He shook his head. "I've never done that before."

"Same here," I said, wondering if I had the guts to reveal my non-existent dating life. "No relationships. Minimal dates." I kept the fact I'd only ever slept with two guys before him to myself.

"Why?" He captured my chin in one hand and tilted my face slightly, studying me. "You're sweet and smart and gorgeous."

Heat flushed my cheeks. "Thanks."

Silence stretched between us and he kept studying me. "You didn't answer my question?"

That's because I had no idea if I was ready to reveal so much of myself to a guy I had no future with.

I wasn't a fool. In a few weeks I'd be heading back to Denver and Kye would stay here, being groomed by my dad before taking the fast-tracked route to tennis stardom. He was that good. My dad knew it. I'd overheard him talking to some of the coaches after Kye's win today. Kye was the one they'd selected to push to the next level ASAP. I was happy for him. He deserved it. But I'd soon become a distant memory, the vacation fling he had when he first arrived in the States, and I didn't want him to realize he meant so much more to me than that.

Because he did. I'd admitted it—albeit to myself—earlier tonight, sometime between the nachos and fajitas we'd shared at my favorite Mexican restaurant, that I'd fallen a little bit in love with Kye.

Not that I knew what loving a guy felt like. But if it was this hollow, tummy-tumbling feeling I constantly had whether I was with him or not, and the amazing warm feeling of being safe and cherished whenever I was with him, then yeah, I think I loved him, just a tad. Because falling any more than that? Lunacy.

I didn't want to head back to Denver with a broken heart.

I tried to ignore the tiny voice inside my head that insisted 'what if it was too late?'

Shadows clouded Kye's eyes and he released my chin. I knew what he was thinking. He'd opened up to me and told me so much of his past, and I couldn't answer a simple question.

"I don't date much because I'm not good with emotions," I said, wondering if it sounded as weak to his ears as it did to mine. "The only guy I've ever loved is my dad. How pathetic is that?"

Tenderness eased the slight frown between his brows. "I think it's kinda cute."

"Cute when I was six and he bought me a toy unicorn. Or when I was eight and he surprised me at Christmas with a pony. But when I'm in my early twenties and my dad is still the number one guy in my life? Not so much."

I huffed out a breath, hoping he couldn't hear the wistfulness in my voice. "The thing is, I didn't see my dad all that much growing up and while I know he loves me, I feel like ... like I can't rely on anyone."

There, I'd said it, voiced my number one fear when it came to relationships, even familial ones: that I couldn't depend on anyone but myself.

"Know what you mean," he said, eyeing me with

newfound respect. "The only person I've ever counted on is me. Easier that way."

I nodded, stunned that we'd found more common ground, when I'd expected him to look at me like I was a freak for feeling alone despite having my dad raise me. "I've made a few good friends at DU, but no one like Dani, who I've grown up with. So apart from her and Dad, I'm a pretty closed off person."

"I don't agree." He snagged one of my hands and lifted it to his lips, brushing soft kisses across my knuckles. "You're cautious, there's a difference." His teeth nipped the base of my thumb and I bit back a groan. "And I'd say you carefully weigh decisions and generally make good choices, but you're hanging out with me, so there goes that theory."

I smiled and reached up to cup his cheek. "What we're doing now? Talking like this? Means a lot to me."

Which was better than what I really wanted to say: means more to me than you could possibly know.

Because that was way too close to the truth. A truth that would ensure he'd keep his distance for the remainder of my vacation if he ever found out. And he wouldn't. Not from me. There was soul-baring and there was soul-baring. I'd shared enough with Kye. I'd take my secret—and my broken heart—back to Denver when the time came.

"Means a lot to me too, babe." He hauled me into his arms and squeezed so hard I could hardly breathe. "Being with you is the smartest thing I've done in a long time."

As he held me tight, I wasn't feeling so smart. In fact, with my feelings for Kye in turmoil, and already dreading our parting when I headed back to DU, I knew I was a dummy for falling in love with my vacation fling.

∼

IT WAS OFFICIAL. I was a love-struck schmuck, as I rolled over in bed and pressed my face into the pillow that still had a trace of Kye on it. Masculine and fresh and spicy, I inhaled deeply, my receptors already pining for him, despite the fact he'd only left ten minutes ago.

We'd been cutting it fine, waiting until dawn for him to head back to his villa, but he'd seemed reluctant to leave and I hadn't wanted him to. If it were up to me, we'd be strutting around the academy hand in hand, proud of our relationship.

But my dad would throw a hissy fit and no way would I put Kye's future on the line. Rolling onto my back and covering my face with Kye's pillow, I ignored the insistent inner voice that said I already had.

We were playing with fire, I knew that. But I was greedy. I wanted as much of Kye as I could get before we parted and if he was willing to take the risk dating me, no way in hell I'd say no.

Selfish? Absolutely. He could lose everything while I'd come out of this relationship unscathed. But I'd be damned if I stopped seeing the first guy I'd truly fallen for. Because this skin-tingling, belly-warming, heart-aching feeling? Was addictive. I wanted more—hell, I wanted it all—for as long as I could get it.

A discreet knock sounded at the door and I leaped out of bed, hoping it was Kye but knowing he'd never risk coming here in daylight.

I quickly pulled on a T-shirt and cotton boxers before opening the door, to find Dani glowering at me.

"Hey, sweetie, what's up?"

"You tell me." She pushed past me without waiting to be invited in and I sighed as I closed the door. I loved my BFF but after the incredible date night I'd had with Kye, I wanted to savor the high, not deal with whatever was Dani's drama of the day.

"Want some OJ—"

"You stood me up last night." Dani swung around so fast I almost slammed into her chest. "Not cool, babe."

"What are you talking about? We didn't have plans ..." I trailed off, belatedly remembering she'd mentioned something about heading into LA when we'd been at the tournament. "Not concrete plans, that is."

Dani's eyes narrowed. "Don't you check your cell anymore? Because I texted you. Five times." She held up a hand, fingers spread. "I don't text my boyfriends that many times for the duration of our relationship, in case you were wondering."

"You have boyfriends?" I tried to lighten the mood, to make her laugh like she usually would when I teased her about the many guys on her speed dial, guys who were fuck buddies and little else.

To my surprise, she shot me a venomous glare that made me take a step back. "I don't appreciate being blown off for some prick you won't see any more in a few weeks."

I rarely lost my temper. But having Dani barge in here, effectively wrecking my post-date glow and flinging around her opinions, sparked my anger.

"What's it to you?" I unclenched my fingers when I realized I'd inadvertently made fists and my fingernails were digging into my palms. "I don't interfere in your *relationships* and I'd appreciate the same courtesy from you."

My emphasis on relationships was a direct dig at her lack of them and she knew it. "Besides, it's what you did to me for years. Choosing some loser to spend the evening with instead of me. Ditching our plans. Being selfish. Not giving a damn about anyone but yourself." The resentment I'd quashed during our teen years spilled out in a torrent that shocked us both.

Dani and I didn't fight. We'd grown up together and she'd been the sibling I never had. But she'd just pushed my buttons in a big way and I felt sick to my stomach that I'd revealed too much. Especially when I saw the sheen of tears in her eyes.

Dani never cried. Not once in all the years we'd been friends had she shed so much as one tear. It made me feel like a bitch.

"Look, just forget it—"

"No." Dani squared her shoulders, her stare icy despite the shimmer of tears. "Feel better, getting that off your chest? Because you've obviously been stewing on it for a decade."

Her upper lip curled in a sneer. "Anything else you want to give me shit for?" She tapped her temple, pretending to think, before snapping her fingers. "I know. Why don't you tell me what you really think about all the guys I've slept with. Just call me a slut and be done with it. Or how you've never forgiven me for not following you to the ass end of the earth and attending DU with you."

Dani's voice had risen with each accusation and rather than making me want to back down, I was spitting mad again. Because the truth was, she'd articulated some of the stuff that *had* bugged me for years, and now that it was finally out in the open, maybe I would get some answers.

"Why do you do it? Sleep with so many guys?"

If I'd scored a direct hit, she didn't show it. Instead, Dani steeled her expression into a hardness I'd never seen. "Who says I sleep with them all?"

It was the first time I'd heard her admit what I often

suspected: that Dani liked to portray herself worse than she was. "You do. It's all you ever did when we were teenagers, boasting about your conquests, taunting the other kids at school into calling you a slut." I shook my head, sadness replacing my anger. "I hated how you belittled yourself like that."

She glanced away, but not before I'd seen a flicker of pain. "It's all in the past."

"Is it?" I pointed at the clubhouse in the distance, visible through the front window. "Because even our first night together, when I wanted to stay in and catch up, all you wanted to do was pick up some random guy." I puffed out a breath. "You're still doing it, Dani. Whenever we're together, all you want to do is hit on guys or rustle up a party or scope your next prey."

That last comment was catty but now that the truth was tumbling out of me, I was on a roll and couldn't stop. "As for you not coming to college with me? That didn't bug me half as much as you not telling me the truth as to why."

Dani sagged a little and I almost went to her. Almost.

"Not everything revolves around you," she said, her tone frigid. "You have your secrets, I have mine."

"What secrets ..."

Damn, if she knew how involved I really was with Kye, there was no telling what she'd do in this mood. Would she betray me to my dad? I sure as hell hoped not.

"I saw the Aussie leave her a little while ago." She pinned me with a stare that meant business. "You should be proud, banging the hottest jock."

I winced at her crudeness and she sniggered.

"Don't worry, your secret's safe with me." She glanced at her watch and faked a yawn. "Pity though. By the time you've finished playing with your newest toy, vacation will be over and we won't have any time to hang out."

She fake-knuckled her eyes. "Boo-fucking-hoo."

I stared in disbelief as the one, true friend I had in the world flipped me the finger and strode toward the door, slamming it on her way out.

TWENTY-TWO
KYE

My morning may have started off pretty frigging great, waking up next to Mia after our first official date night, but the day had gone downhill from there.

Despite a positive game analysis from Dirk, where he'd ripped apart every forehand, backhand and serve in my last match, highlighting the good, encouraging where I could improve, I'd been on edge.

I didn't like lies and sitting next to Dirk for two hours while he gave me tips to take my game to the next level made me feel like a first-grade prick.

He'd warned me off his daughter. And I didn't give a shit. Not sure when the truth hit. Sometime between him praising my third return in the fourth game of the second set and Dirk suggesting I come to LA to meet with some of his old sponsors next week. I should've been over the moon. Sponsors meant money. Money meant security. Security meant following my dream of being the best.

But was it? Was playing in Grand Slams really my dream? Or had this game I'd first played to blow off steam snowballed into much more than I wanted?

I liked tennis. Tennis was good for me. It kept me centered and focused and the darkness at bay. But since I'd met Mia I'd realized that anger didn't need to fuel my tennis. I could win without it. The million-dollar question was, did I want to?

Because sometime during Dirk's analysis, I'd realized that I wasn't hungry enough. Winning Grand Slams wasn't the be-all and end-all for me. Initially I'd used tennis as a release, lately as a way to pay back my dad and hopefully gain his respect.

Now? It didn't seem to matter so much. Talking with Mia, tapping into feelings I hadn't known existed, made me see that I didn't need to play tennis to be a halfway decent human being.

I could do that on my own.

All I had to figure out was how to break it to Dad and where did that leave my future?

I entered my villa and dumped my workout bag near the door, spying a folded piece of paper that had been slipped under it.

I picked it up and opened it, unable to stop a stupid grin as I saw who'd written it.

EVERYONE ATTENDING CLUBHOUSE DINNER AT 6.
MEET ME AT THE POOLHOUSE.

Considering how fired up we'd got at the pool house last time, I couldn't wait to meet Mia there. Maybe I could discuss the stuff bouncing around my head, see what she thought. She'd been amazingly insightful so far and the crazy thing was, I couldn't imagine talking to anyone else about my private thoughts the way I did with her.

I knew this thing we had would end when she went back to uni and I figured out what the hell I wanted to do that didn't involve following a futile dream here at the academy. But I'd never expected to feel this ... sad, at the thought of not having her around anymore.

A quick glance at the digi clock on the counter showed I had ten minutes to shower and meet Mia. Ten more minutes to mull answers to questions I was too scared to contemplate let alone want to acknowledge.

Questions like, how would I extricate myself from the deal I'd made with my dad? How could I leave the academy without pissing off Dirk and ultimately affecting my chances with Mia? And the biggie, why the hell was I even considering a future with Mia beyond her holiday fling?

No amount of vigorous shampooing or hot water cleared my head and as I headed for the pool house I couldn't help but hope things would be clearer once I saw Mia.

As corny as it sounded, everything seemed better when I was around her.

The pool house was in darkness, bar the solar-powered lights that ringed the pool. Perfect place for a secret assignation, as I'd found out the first time she'd followed me here.

The chlorine-tinged humidity engulfed me as I entered. "Babe, you in here?"

Silence, punctuated by the soft hum of the filter. Wishing she'd get here already, I sank onto one of the sun loungers and lay back, hands behind my head, legs outstretched.

I hadn't had much downtime since I'd arrived here. Every minute of every day was taken up by practice or team meetings or lectures from the sport scientists/psychologists/exercise physiologists. And when I wasn't on the court,

I was expected to schmooze with my fellow academy wannabes. The rest of the time? I'd been with Mia. And that's what I wanted more of.

My eyes drifted shut as I imagined what we could've been like if we'd met under different circumstances. What it would be like to date her.

She was quirky and funny and beautiful, inside and out. I'd never met anyone like her. And I'd miss her more than I cared to admit.

"Glad you came, Big Boy."

My eyes snapped open in time to see Dani straddle me, lean forward and kiss me.

It took my befuddled brain several seconds to process what the fuck was going on and by the time I sat up, grabbed her waist to haul her off and wrenched my mouth away, it was too late.

Mia stood outside the glass door to the pool house, staring at me like I'd stabbed her in the heart.

"Get the fuck off me," I growled, shoving Dani away, not caring when she sprawled on the cold tiles at my feet. "What kind of a sick bitch comes onto her friend's guy?"

"The worst kind," she murmured, the bleakness in her eyes not stopping me from stepping over her on my way to Mia.

However, by the time I glanced up, Mia had gone.

TWENTY-THREE

MIA

I ran.

Ran as fast as I could, channeling every ounce of pain and devastation into my feet, willing them to take me as far from the ugliness as I could get.

I had no idea where I was headed, until I reached the main house. This was where I could hide. Regroup. My sanctuary.

I let myself in the back door and bounded up the steps, taking them two at a time, needing the safety of my old bedroom, the one place in this topsy-turvy world I'd always felt safe.

I burst into the room, half expecting it to be converted into another of my dad's trophy rooms. Instead, it was like entering a time warp. Nothing had changed. Nothing. The queen size bed covered in a pink satin throw. The dressing table covered in hairbrushes and make-up and jewelry. The bookcase stacked to overflowing, paperbacks and hardbacks jostling for position three-deep. The corkboard covered in postcards from around the world, from every city my dad played in.

The familiarity drew me in, comforted, as I locked the door, crossed to the bed, and dove under the covers. Where I lay for the next two hours, alternating between crying my eyes out and formulating my plan.

I had to leave tonight; there was no question of staying.

And I couldn't see Kye, that was a given.

Kye.

The guy I'd fallen in love with.

The guy who'd been kissing my best friend.

The guy who'd been lying, cheating scum.

God, I was such a fool.

Had he been playing me all along? I didn't think so, but then, what did I know? With no relationship experience, a guy like him could tell me anything and I'd believe him.

Shit, I had. Believed it all. Every single word he'd fed me.

Had it all been a lie? Or was he tired of me and suring up his bet for once I left? Maybe that was it: Dani would be around once I headed back to Denver and he wanted to move from one girl to another.

As for Dani, nothing she did surprised me anymore. We'd been growing apart for years and our fight had cemented what I'd known for a while. We had nothing in common any more. I was working hard at college to make it on my own. Dani was living off her trust fund, drinking and partying and sleeping her way around LA.

And apparently, she'd decided to sleep with my boyfriend.

The pain gutted me anew, like someone had stuck a knife in my stomach and ripped upward, leaving a jagged, gaping hole leading directly to my heart. It ached with a fierceness that made me gasp for air.

I had to escape. Tonight. Without arousing Dad's suspicions and ensuring Kye kept out of my way.

In the end, it was too easy. The simplicity of my plan would guarantee success.

But it all hinged on one thing: me being able to pull off the biggest con job of the century.

That I was a perfectly normal girl eager to get back to college to help out a friend in need. A girl who hadn't just had her heart torn in two by an absolute bastard.

∼

I KNEW Dad's official clubhouse dinners took three hours, so I texted him to meet me at the house when he was done and spent a good thirty minutes making myself presentable. Washed my face. Practiced smiling in front of the mirror. It didn't look like a grimace and I almost believed I could pull this off, until I saw my eyes. Dull. Lifeless. Empty. Like a light had been switched off.

I blinked several times, trying to erase the devastation. It didn't work, but hopefully Dad would be preoccupied as usual and wouldn't notice. Wouldn't be the first time.

I heard the front door open and close, and took a few more seconds to compose myself before heading for the den, where I knew Dad would be pouring a post-dinner scotch.

He never invited people up to the main house, something I relied on as I knocked once before entering.

"Hey Dad, how was dinner?"

"Same old," he said, not looking up from the glass in one hand, crystal decanter in the other. "What did you do tonight?"

Saw two people I care about betray me. Had my heart broken. Just your average evening. Not.

"Stayed in, grabbed a sandwich while I watched a movie." Thankfully, my voice didn't quiver at all. Good. I could do this. "'Til I got a call from my roommate, and then I packed."

He glanced up, a frown creasing his brow. "Packed?"

"I'm heading back to Denver tonight, Dad." Mustering my best hangdog expression, I sat on the leather sofa, trying to appear relaxed. "Andie's having a few problems and needs my help."

His frown deepened. "What kind of problems?"

I played my trump card. "Woman's problems." Two words guaranteed to strike fear into the heart of any male.

Predictably, my dad appeared uncomfortable as he sat behind his desk and downed half his scotch in one gulp. "Doesn't she have family?"

"Her folks are in Canada helping her other sister, who's just given birth to her first child."

"And she has no one else?"

"Dad, she wouldn't have called if she did." I sighed, throwing in a minor lower lip wobble. "I have to go help her."

After a long pause, he nodded. "Sure, sweetheart. Guess I'm just grumpy because this cuts your vacation short."

"I know, Dad, but I'll be back at the end of next semester, before you know it." I stood, crossed the room and bent to hug him. "Love you."

"Love you too, baby girl." He stood and hugged me tight, the type of hug I wish he'd been around to give a lot more often when I'd been growing up. "Do you need me to charter a jet for you?"

"Would you?" I'd been counting on this too. A speedy getaway facilitated by my dad who had influence and money and got things done.

"Absolutely." He disengaged from our hug, already reaching for the phone.

"Thanks." Time to add the one thing guaranteed to ensure I escaped without seeing Kye. "Oh, I almost forgot. I ran into Kye on the way up here. Said he'd missed dinner because he was practicing some of the strokes you'd given him feedback on, and he wanted to discuss it further with you tonight. Said he'd be in his villa."

"Okay, thanks honey, I'll go see him once I've arranged everything for you."

"You're the best." I blew him a kiss and slipped out of the den, making my way back up to my old bedroom, where I had the perfect vantage point to wait and watch.

My cell beeped. Dad, sending me all the deets of my departure. Which would be accelerated if the rest of the plan I set in motion happened.

I waited a long five minutes before I saw Kye heading toward the house, no doubt in search of me, and Dad met him halfway, guiding him toward the gymnasium where he'd hopefully spend the next hour at least dissecting Kye's strokes.

My chance to escape.

I bolted from the house toward my villa, where I threw things into a suitcase, stuffed my overnight bag with things I'd need on the jet and grabbed a water bottle. By that time, the limo had pulled up outside.

Like clockwork.

As I slid into the limo's cool leather interior, I risked one last glance at the gym. No Kye in sight. Good. I'd done it.

Then why did I feel so goddamned bad?

TWENTY-FOUR
KYE

I knew it had been too good to be true.

Happiness didn't happen to schmucks like me. I should be used to it. Every single time I'd been happy in my life, something had happened to fuck it up. Losing Mum. Losing the only home I'd ever known. And now, losing Mia.

Our time together may have been short but it had been so worth it. For the first time in a long time, I'd been truly happy. Which of course meant it had to go belly-up.

To make matters worse, I had to abort my frantic search for her when Dirk collared me and dragged me to the gym to discuss my strokes. Strokes that I'd been practicing through dinner, apparently, according to Mia.

Smart move, setting her dad onto me, buying time to cool down. Because I could imagine how furious she must be. To walk in and see her bestie kissing me ... this was such a fuck-up. I had to find her ASAP and explain.

After a long two hours with Dirk, I bolted to her villa and banged on the door. Checked my mobile for the umpteenth time. Fired off another desperate text for her to contact me. And banged on the door some more.

"She's not there."

I jumped and spun around, to find Pete eyeing me with speculation. Great, last thing I needed was this shithead witnessing anything between Mia and I, so I feigned nonchalance. "Do you know where she is?"

"Gone back to Denver. Some emergency with her roommate." Pete shrugged and made loco circles at his temple. "Couldn't think of anything worse, cutting vacation short to head back to college early."

I could think of worse things. Like the girl I loved running out on me because she thought I was a low-life bastard.

"Yeah," I said, making a grand show of looking at my watch. "I'm beat. See you at practice in the morning."

As if. I wouldn't be here in the morning. I'd be on the first plane to Denver.

"Too bad, huh?" Pete smirked. "Looks like I wasn't the only one who wanted to nail Coach's daughter."

I could hit him. I should hit him. But the anger that would normally flood me in situations like this didn't come.

Sure, I still wanted to dropkick this dickhead for being a sleaze, but the darkness that usually descended? Vanished. Just like the woman who'd helped banish it.

"Whatever." I gave Pete the two-fingered salute and headed back to my villa.

I needed time to think, to plan, to research.

I knew one thing. If I went after Mia, my tennis career was finished.

Dirk wouldn't take kindly to his latest protégé absconding. He'd be royally pissed off. And he'd tell my dad.

Chasing after Mia would mean effectively screwing up my last chance. The thought should've had me terrified. Instead, all I could think was, 'what if I told Dad first?'

Because that's what I'd have to do. He'd stood by me too many times for me to blow him off for love.

Love?

Fuck, that's the second time in as many minutes I'd associated love with Mia.

I loved her.

Me. A guy who barely knew the meaning of the word. Pity my timing sucked.

When I reached my villa, I paced for a good ten minutes. Formulating ideas. Discarding. Refining. And not once in all that time did I feel bad about walking away from my tennis career.

Guess I had my answer right there.

Being at the academy, in Sydney and here, had never been about a great passion for the game. It had been about me escaping, running away, doing whatever it took to avoid a lot of the painful crap in my life.

Thanks to Mia, I was through running.

I knew what I wanted. Her. And if that meant being in Denver, I'd do it.

But I needed help first.

Doing a quick calculation of time differences between here and Sydney, I fired up my laptop to call Dad.

It took several seconds for his face to appear on the screen, a big smile creasing the face that most Australians knew and loved as the face of talk show.

"Hey, Son, how's life in Cali?"

I settled for a noncommittal "Okay."

"Doesn't look it, by that frown." Dad mimicked a gloomy expression. "What's on your mind?"

Here went nothing.

"I want to quit tennis. Not entirely, but I don't want to play the professional circuit. I want to go to college. In

Denver. Enroll in an English major. Play college tennis for fun, not out of obligation to repay your faith in me."

The words tumbled out in a rush, the half-formed ideas that I'd toyed with coalescing into a plan that sounded crazy but doable. "Tennis has been my crutch, Dad. My go-to place for years, a way to burn off my anger. But I've met someone and she's made me realize a lot of stuff and I'm not so angry anymore."

I took a deep breath and rushed on, encouraged by the lack of horror on Dad's face. "You've been amazing, standing by me and pulling strings to get me this second chance. And the last thing I want to do is disappoint you. But I'm hoping you'll be proud of me now, of the decisions I've made, and the way I've learned there's more to life than whacking the shit out of a ball from frustration."

There, I'd said it. A jumbled confession of sorts that should've left me feeling empty. Instead, I felt liberated.

I held my breath, waiting for Dad to speak. When he did, by the admiration glowing in his eyes, I knew everything would be okay.

"I'm proud of you, Son. More than you could ever know." He smiled. "It takes guts to throw away your crutches. Real courage." He made a fist and pumped it in the air. "You're a champ, whether you play tennis or not."

"Thanks, Dad." To my horror, I could feel tears stinging my eyes. "You've never let me down."

Dad's smile faded. "Sadly, that's not true." He shook his head. "I let you down before you were even born."

"You didn't know about me."

The second Dad locked gazes with me and I glimpsed a flicker of guilt, I knew the truth.

"That's the thing, Son. I did know. I knew your mum was pregnant and I accepted her decision to abort." His eyes clouded with pain that must've been reflected in mine. "I could've stuck around and supported her through it, but I didn't. I took the easy way out, was relieved in fact she didn't want me around anymore. So I thought there was no baby." He pressed a hand to his heart. "Finding out I had a son all those years later was a gift, but it also made me terribly ashamed of how I'd walked away too easily all those years earlier."

His shoulders sagged. "Your mum deserved better and so did you."

I hesitated, wanting to ask a question but not entirely certain I wanted to hear the answer. "Is that why you've stood by me these last few years? Out of guilt?"

"Partially," he admitted. "But I could see so much of myself in you, how I was at your age, that I hoped you needed a father as much as I'd needed one but never had."

I admired Dad's honesty and was more than a little intrigued. "So you took your frustrations out on a tennis ball too?"

"Nothing so harmless." A wry smile alleviated some of the tension pinching his mouth. "I was a dumb bastard who took my frustration at life out on a bottle and pot." He screwed up his nose. "When I wasn't stoned I was blind drunk, seeking solace in something, anything, rather than face my miserable existence. Thank God you were smarter than that."

"Yeah, so smart I busted a guy's nose."

"Better than busting into a liquor store and stealing."

Dad's admission hung in the air until I closed my gaping jaw.

"I was shady, kid. A real dumb-arse. At least you were smart enough to channel your anger into sport." He pointed at me. "But I knew there'd come a time you wouldn't need to depend on tennis anymore and looks like that time has come."

"So you're not mad or disappointed?"

He shook his head. "I eventually worked through my rough stuff and I knew you'd do the same. Mad? I'm bloody proud." Dad glanced away from the screen for a moment and when he looked back at me, I'd never seen him look so uncertain. "I never wanted to be one of those parents who told kids what to do. I felt like I'd never earned the right. So I watched you fight and struggle against your anger the same way I had, but you were so much smarter than me. You were street-wise and savvy and knew how to control it." He gently fist-bumped the screen. "I've led an interesting life, filled with good and bad. But finding out I had a son, then being privileged enough to get to know you and be a father you can turn to, is the best thing that's ever happened to me."

"Thanks, Dad." I fist-bumped the screen right back at him, swallowing the urge to bawl like a baby. "Just so you know, Dirk's going to throw a shit-fit when he finds out I've gone after Mia, because he already warned me off her and doesn't know we're dating."

Dad's eyes widened, before a slow grin spread across his face. "You're dating Dirk's daughter?"

I nodded and Dad laughed. "Dirk's always been a smug bastard, even if he's one of the good guys." He winked. "Leave it to me, Son. I'll take care of Dirk while you go after your girl."

Your girl ... I liked the sound of that.

"You wouldn't happen to have any friends in high places at the University of Denver, would you? Because I sure could do with some string-pulling like you did with Dirk."

Dad nodded. "Leave it with me. One of my producers

has a son-in-law who's on the faculty at some uni in Denver. I'll follow it up."

"You're the best, Dad."

And I meant it. I may not have had a father growing up, but he'd stepped up when I needed him most. I was one lucky son of a bitch.

"Right back at you, kid." He ended our session with a salute and as I closed the laptop, I was one step closer to achieving my goal.

Finding Mia.

Convincing her I loved her.

And sticking around for the long haul.

TWENTY-FIVE
MIA

Two hours after I entered my dorm and indulged in another bout of useless weeping, Dani showed up.

She didn't knock, just barged into my room like she owned the place.

I sat up and pointed at the door. "Fuck off."

She didn't move. Not a flicker of a muscle. Not a blink. If she'd responded with her characteristic smart-ass attitude or apologized or even groveled, I would probably have physically manhandled her and thrown her out.

Instead, I stared in shock as Dani did the one thing she'd never done in front of me.

Cry.

Tears ran down her cheeks, her eerily blank expression scaring me as much as the way she was staring at me: like someone had just died.

"Here." I handed her a box of tissues and tried not to feel sorry for her.

My best friend had betrayed me in the worst possible way and if she thought a few tears would gain my forgiveness, she was wrong.

She took the box and sank onto the floor, legs tucked under her as she leaned against the desk, the way she used to do when we were kids and swapping stories on our latest crushes in my room. We'd talk for hours, only stopping to nibble on peanut butter cookies and down lemonade prepared by the nanny. We'd braid each other's hair and paint our toenails and scribble secrets into our journals, before proceeding to spill every one of those secrets.

Without a mom, Dani had been the main female influence in my life. I'd adored her, every loud, rambunctious, bossy inch of her. But no amount of precious memories could erase what she'd done today.

I didn't speak, because I knew if I started I'd end up screaming. So I sat and waited for her to dry her eyes and blow her nose, quelling the sympathy that continued to well up as I realized how awful she looked.

Dani never left the house without make-up and her hair blow-dried to sleek perfection. She wore skimpy designer gear with the sole intent to be noticed wherever she went. She never looked like this: blotchy red skin, bloodshot eyes, lank hair snagged in two pigtails and saggy grey yoga pants with a matching sloppy joe.

When she finally opened her mouth to speak, I braced myself.

"I know you want to slap me from here into oblivion and I don't blame you, but I'm really hoping you'll hear me out," she said, wringing her hands. "Please."

I didn't want to listen to her trite apology but I shrugged my agreement. Short of physically dragging her toward the door and shoving her through it, I knew she wouldn't leave until she appeased her conscience.

"I'm sorry, Mia, for everything. For being a jealous bitch that you found happiness with a guy in such a short space of time. For wanting to hurt you as much as you hurt me for blowing me off. For deliberately setting you up ..." She shook her head and a lone tear rolled down her cheek. "I left a note for Kye, saying you'd meet him at the pool house, and I did the same to you. I wanted you to see me come onto him."

Anger churned my gut as she continued. "Kye didn't even know I was there. He was waiting for you, lying on a lounger, eyes closed. I hid 'til I saw you approaching the pool house and I jumped his bones."

Her breath hitched in a part-sob, part-hiccup, and my fingers curled into fists so I wouldn't strangle her.

"He pushed me off straight away, but I'd achieved what I set out to do when I saw you standing there ... fuck, I'm so sorry." She absentmindedly shredded tissues, twisting them into tiny pieces. "People have ignored me my whole life. Friends, family, but never you. That's why I used to act like I put out so much in high school, to get noticed. But you were the only person who saw the real me, who paid me any attention. And when you didn't I kinda snapped." She made crazy circles at her temple. "It's no excuse, I know, but I wanted you to know you're the only person I can really depend on in this world and I'd never deliberately hurt you if I was thinking straight."

"But you did hurt me." I leaped off the bed and stood, towering over her. "Don't you get it, Dani? You've crossed a line. I trusted you and now we can't ever go back. And you've screwed my relationship with Kye in the process."

Damn, the tears I'd been holding in stung the back of my eyes. Pressing the pads of my fingers to my eyes, I murmured, "Just go."

I could hear her sobs but I couldn't bear to look at her. Thanks to Dani, I'd run out on Kye. I'd believed what I'd seen and hadn't believed enough in him. Or myself. What we'd had was real and I'd allowed Dani to tarnish it.

"Look, there's nothing you can say that can mend our friendship so please leave—"

"I lost the baby."

Dani had spoken so softly I could've sworn I must've imagined her whisper.

I lowered my hands and opened my eyes, to find her staring at me with a bleakness that stabbed me in the chest.

"That's what the nurse said. 'You've lost the baby'." She grimaced, as if in pain. "Like I'd ever lose something, someone, so precious."

Stunned, I sank onto the floor in front of her. I wanted to ask a billion questions but waited for her to continue. She looked like she was in a trance, reciting the truth like an automaton.

"That's why I couldn't come here with you." She gestured around the room. "I wanted to attend college with you so badly, but I got pregnant. Didn't tell my flaky folks, not that they would've noticed 'til I was about to deliver anyway."

Her legs unfolded and she stretched them out in front, rested her hands in her lap now she'd finally stopped massacring tissues. "I was happy, truly happy, for the first time in my life. I thought a baby would fill the emptiness I've always felt. You know my parents. You know the life I've led. Glamorous on the outside, fake on the inside. A baby would've been all mine, would've had to pay me attention ..."

I wanted to say something but had no idea what. Dani's revelation had floored me, and semi-cracked the barriers I'd erected around my heart.

That had been the start of the end for us, when she'd

decided not to come to college with me and made up that lame excuse about having the flu. Deep down, I'd never forgiven her and we'd been drifting apart ever since.

Knowing the truth, the explosive truth, went some way to healing the rift.

"You were always my voice of reason, Mia. My adorably strait-laced best friend. And that's why I didn't tell even you." She blinked as more tears fell. "Because I was scared you'd talk me out of keeping the baby. Because I was terrified you'd say all the logical things I probably needed to hear and I'd end up resenting you for it."

She puffed out a long breath. "So I didn't tell a soul. Then I miscarried at twelve weeks. And I spent the next three years trying to numb the pain by partying hard and sleeping around and doing too many dumbass things."

Dani knuckled her eyes, before her gaze locked on mine with startling clarity. "What I did to you? Trying to hurt you by ruining your relationship with Kye? It's the last straw. I've been on a downward spiral for too long. Losing this?" She waved her hand between us. "Losing us? Has made me realize I need to stop. So I'm leaving. Going overseas for a while. Anywhere but LA, so I can get my shit together."

She stood slowly, struggling to her feet like an old woman. "But I had to tell you the truth before I left. Because even now, a part of me hopes that one day you'll forgive me and we can be friends again."

She held her hands out to me, to help me off the floor.

I had two choices. Hold onto my resentment and let her walk out of here. Or understand and forgive and get my best friend back.

I placed my hands in hers and she tugged me up so hard I stumbled. Fell against her. And then we were hugging and sniveling and crying.

"I'm so sorry you went through all that alone," I said, when we finally stopped embracing and released each other.

"Thanks, it was tough." Dani plucked the last tissue out of the box, tore it in two, and handed me half. "Gutted me. Which is why I went a little crazy."

I managed a wobbly smile. "What was your excuse before?"

"Bitch," she said, and we laughed.

Her smile faded all too quickly. "Are you going to talk to Kye? Because I really think you should." She grimaced. "I'm so ashamed of my behavior. I'll apologize to him too and then you can work things out—"

"I'm scared," I murmured, recognizing the truth a second after the words tumbled from my lips. "I've fallen in love for the first time with a guy I barely know. A guy who's going to be travelling the world and meeting gorgeous women and who I wasn't going to see after the end of vacation anyway, so what's the point ..." I trailed off, having articulated my deepest fears when it came to Kye.

I wasn't a fool. Once the initial pain from seeing Dani on top of him had faded, I'd known why I'd run. Because I'd avoided the inevitable break-up we faced. I'd taken the easy way out. So why did it now feel so hard?

"Want to know what I think?"

"You're going to tell me anyway," I said, incredibly thankful to have my opinionated BFF back.

Dani managed a wobbly smile. "If you love him, fight for him. Don't let a possible cloudy future dictate what you could have today."

She squeezed my arm. "At least, that's what I used to help me decide whether to keep the baby or not. I was terrified, imagining how someone like me could care for a baby. I concocted terrible scenarios in my head, each worse than the last. But when it came down to it?" She shrugged, but I glimpsed the incredible pain of loss in her eyes. "I would've rather lived my life with my baby than give it away for fear of a future that may never happen."

"Aww, honey ..." I hugged her again, swiftly and fiercely, releasing her before we started to bawl again. "Thanks. You've really helped."

"Glad to."

A knock sounded at the door and I glanced at my watch in surprise. Even if most students weren't away on vacation, I wouldn't normally have visitors at three a.m.

When I opened the door, my heart stopped.

"Don't you ever leave me again," Kye said, a second before he hauled me into his arms and squeezed so tight like he'd never let go.

I wished.

What seemed like an eternity later, Kye released me.

Dani brushed past us. "I'm sorry, Kye. I was an idiot in Santa Monica." She slung an arm around my shoulder. "Mia will explain everything." She squeezed me and pecked me on the cheek. "Take care, hon. I'll be in touch."

"Okay." I waited until Dani left before hauling Kye inside and slamming the door shut. There was so much to say and I had no freaking idea where to start.

"Nothing happened—"

"Sorry for running—"

We spoke simultaneously, both halting at the same time, followed by nervous laughter. When Kye took a seat at my desk, I chose the bed. I couldn't be near him to have this conversation, because if he touched me again I'd fall into his arms without needing what had to be said.

"You first," I said, chicken to the end.

He braced his elbows on his knees, making his navy T-shirt pull taut across his delts and upper back. A back I'd scoured in ecstasy. A back I wanted to wrap my arms around even now and never let go.

"Nothing happened between Dani and me. She came onto me, I shoved her away. That's it." He sucked in a breath and blew it out. "I don't give a flying fuck about any other woman because you're the one I want."

No declaration of love. Good. It would make this easier.

"Dani told me what happened, how she wrote us both notes, then deliberately came onto you to pay me back for abandoning her in favor of you."

He made loopy circles at his head. "Your friend's seriously whacko."

"She's been through a lot. Stuff I didn't know about." I shrugged. "But we've cleared the air and we'll be okay."

"Can you say the same about us?" He stood so abruptly the chair slammed into the desk. "I thought we had something, Mia. Something good. So how could you believe I'd be screwing around on you and then run before giving me a chance to explain?"

I needed to tell him a semi-truth before I said the rest.

"I was hurt. Devastated. Because I thought we'd been good together too." I pressed a hand to my chest where even now, the pain spiked at the memory of how shattered I'd been when I saw him and Dani together. "I needed to get away. Back to reality."

His eyes narrowed. "You're saying what we had wasn't real?"

I hadn't expected him to read between the lines so quickly. That was my man, smart and gorgeous. Though he wasn't my man any more. Not after tonight.

Hoping I could do this without breaking down in a

blubbering mess, I nodded. "People hook up on vacations all the time. Incredibly intense flings that suck you in at the time, but when it inevitably ends, as it has to, you realize it was nothing more than a romantic fantasy." I was so proud when my voice didn't wobble.

"Bullshit," he said, starting to pace, stopping every few seconds to glare at me. "We had more than that."

I sat on my hands to stop them from shaking and giving away how nervous I was. "It was fun, Kye. And the sex was phenomenal. But it was always going to end."

Damn, the pain was back again, slicing my heart and making me breathless.

"What if it didn't have to end?" He stopped in front of me and knelt at my feet, placing his hands either side of me on the bed, effectively trapping me. "Would that shitty little speech you just gave change?"

My mouth gaped for a second before I closed it, hating how my heart gave a betraying leap of hope. "It has to end. We both knew that going into this."

"Things change." He leaned forward and laid his cheek on my knee. "I've changed."

He said it so softly I had to lean down a little to hear him.

"What do you mean?" I held my breath, knowing there was nothing he could say that would alter the outcome but too weak to push him away when I'd never seen him this vulnerable.

He lifted his head and looked me straight in the eye. "I want to be with you. Here. At DU."

The blood must've drained from my face because a sudden chill made me shiver. This couldn't be real.

Had Kye just said what I thought he'd said?

"Hey, don't faint on me." He straightened from a squat

position to sit next to me. "Not quite the reaction I'd expected."

"But you can't stay here." I shook my head, trying to clear the fog. "You're going to be a Grand Slam champion one day."

"I'd rather be your champion." He slid an arm around my waist and held me tight. "The thing is, I've gone and fallen in love with you. And it turns out I don't need tennis as badly as I need you."

I turned to face him, slowly, not daring to hope. "You love me?"

"Yeah, go figure." He kissed me to prove it, a hard, fast kiss filled with desperation. Like he couldn't get enough. Like he was petrified he wouldn't get another.

I pushed him away before we ended up how we usually ended up after a kiss: naked and entangled and incredibly satisfied.

"I can't let you give up tennis for me." When he opened his mouth to speak, I pressed my fingers against it. "You'd end up resenting me. And I'd end up hating myself for it."

I lowered my hand, leaned forward and brushed a soft kiss across his lips. "You're an amazing guy and I'll miss you a lot, but you can't do this."

He captured my face in his hands. "Do you love me?"

I glanced away and compressed my lips.

"Answer the question, Mia." His thumbs caressed my cheeks and I bit back a moan. "Look at me and tell me the truth."

Damn.

I dragged my gaze back to meet his, ready to lie to the man I loved. But what I saw made me crumple.

Kye had tears in his eyes.

He'd put his heart on the line, was risking it all, for me.

The least I owed him before he walked away was the truth.

"Of course I frikking love you," I said, tension gripping my chest like a vice. "But I'm not going to let you throw away your future because of me."

To my surprise, he grinned. "You are my future, you crazy girl." He swooped in for another kiss, softer this time, and I savored the taste of mint on my tongue, the scent of his citrus aftershave filling my senses. "You know tennis was my go-to place, my emotional crutch."

He squared his shoulders, the sheen of tears gone. "But I don't need it anymore."

He winked. "I'm all grown up. And I got there because of you."

He stood, snagged my hands and tugged me to my feet. "I spoke to my dad. He's going to pull strings to get me in here. English major. And I'll play college tennis." He lifted my hand to his mouth and kissed the back of it. "So you're not getting rid of me that easily, babe."

I couldn't believe this. Any of it.

Kye was staying and we had a future?

My knees wobbled and I sunk onto the bed.

"Why are you on the verge of passing out every time I mention we have a future together?" He sat next to me again. "A long, happy future, in case you were wondering."

Emotion clogged my throat and I swallowed, several times, before I could speak. "This is for real? You and me?"

"Always."

As Kye's strong arms slid around me and we hugged like we'd never let go, I finally believed him.

READ TOWING THE LINE, DANI'S STORY, NOW!

I NEED A NEW START. *Anonymity. In a country where no one will know me, and the havoc I create. Not all the rumors about me are true. But I made one mistake too many in LA and attending an Australian college for a few semesters is the perfect solution.*

I plan on avoiding guys. But the part-time tutor and sexy Aussie artist Ashton? Has me re-evaluating the wisdom of being a reformed bad girl. Ash is aloof, dedicated, serious, and I must corrupt him. So I seduce him. Not expecting to fall in love for the first time. And the last.

Because Ash has high standards and when he learns the truth about me, he'll join the long list of people in my life pretending I don't exist.

FREE BOOK AND MORE

SIGN UP TO NICOLA'S NEWSLETTER for a free book!

Read Nicola's newest feel-good romance **DID NOT FINISH**

Or her new gothics **THE RETREAT** and **THE HAVEN**

Try the **CARTWRIGHT BROTHERS** duo

FASCINATION

PERFECTION

The **WORKPLACE LIAISONS** duo

THE BOSS

THE CEO

Try the **BASHFUL BRIDES** series

NOT THE MARRYING KIND

NOT THE ROMANTIC KIND

NOT THE DARING KIND

NOT THE DATING KIND

The **CREATIVE IN LOVE** series

THE GRUMPY GUY

THE SHY GUY

THE GOOD GUY

Try the **BOMBSHELLS** series

BEFORE (FREE!)

BRASH

BLUSH

BOLD

BAD

BOMBSHELLS BOXED SET

The **WORLD APART** series

WALKING THE LINE (FREE!)

CROSSING THE LINE

TOWING THE LINE

BLURRING THE LINE

WORLD APART BOXED SET

The **HOT ISLAND NIGHTS** duo

WICKED NIGHTS

WANTON NIGHTS

The **BOLLYWOOD BILLIONAIRES** series

FAKING IT

MAKING IT

The **LOOKING FOR LOVE** series

LUCKY LOVE

CRAZY LOVE

SAPPHIRES ARE A GUY'S BEST FRIEND

THE SECOND CHANCE GUY

Check out Nicola's website for a full list of her books.

And read her other romances as Nikki North.

'MILLIONAIRE IN THE CITY' series.

LUCKY

COCKY

CRAZY

FANCY

FLIRTY

FOLLY

MADLY

Check out the **ESCAPE WITH ME** series.

DATE ME

LOVE ME

DARE ME

TRUST ME

FORGIVE ME

Try the **LAW BREAKER** series
THE DEAL MAKER
THE CONTRACT BREAKER

EXCERPT FROM TOWING THE LINE

DANI

"Where's Loverboy?"

Not that I really cared where Mia's boyfriend Kye was. I was enjoying having my BFF all to myself for a few hours before I boarded a plane to Australia to start my new life.

"He'll be here soon," Mia said, shoving the half-empty pizza box in my direction. "Said he had to see a man about a dog."

I helped myself to another slice of pepperoni, even though I'd barely nibbled the first. "What the hell does that mean?"

Mia shrugged. "Who knows? I just nod and smile when he comes out with those indecipherable Aussie-isms." Her eyes lit up. "Besides, who cares when he's that cute?"

"Fair enough," I said, eternally grateful we could actually talk like this considering I'd recently fucked up majorly by coming onto Kye with the intention of deliberately hurting Mia.

I'd been acting like the attention-seeking idiot I was and thankfully, Mia and Kye had forgiven me.

I'd told Mia the truth. Well, most of it.

She knew about the baby, why I'd blown off college and why I'd spent the last three years drifting through a haze of partying to forget.

But she didn't know all of it.

Nobody did.

And I intended on keeping it that way.

Sensing my sudden reticence, Mia pushed her plate away and placed a hand on my arm. "You okay?"

I nodded, swallowing the unexpected lump of emotion in my throat. I never got sentimental. Ever. I'd given up being that vulnerable a long time ago. Because feelings led to pain and I never wanted to feel as bad as I did when that bitch of a nurse told me I'd 'lost' my baby.

Like I'd lose anything so precious.

"Guess the reality of leaving all this to attend college in Melbourne for a while has finally hit home." I gestured at the lavish lounge in my parents' Beverly Hills mansion. "I mean, how will I live without the ten widescreens, daily fresh sushi and thousand-thread count toilet paper?"

Mia laughed. "I hear they have two-thousand thread count in Australia." She winked. "How do you think Aussie guys have such hot asses?"

I chuckled, relieved the urge to bawl had receded.

"Talking about me?" Kye Sheldon strode into the room. Tall, blue-eyed, broad-shouldered, he was seriously hot and only had eyes for Mia as he made a beeline for his girlfriend and laid a hot, open-mouthed kiss on her right in front of me.

"Get a room," I muttered, actually enjoying the sight of my best friend being cherished in the way she deserved.

And Mia did deserve it. She'd always been good and why she'd hung out with me for the last fifteen years was beyond me. She was loyal, sweet and trusting. My voice of reason, I'd always called her. Which is why I hadn't told her about the baby.

Because when it came down to it, when I'd fallen pregnant at eighteen, I hadn't wanted to hear all the logical reasons why I shouldn't keep the baby. For the first time in my life, I would've had someone in my life to love me unconditionally. Someone to depend on me. Someone whose world revolved around me.

I'd never had that before. My parents pretended like their only child didn't exist. Too busy living an A-list Hollywood lifestyle in their suck-up job as agents to the stars.

Friends? Non-existent, discounting Mia, who had lived next door until her dad quit professional tennis to open his teaching academy in Santa Monica, and they'd moved. Mia had been my rock for so long. And I'd almost lost her through my own stupidity.

It had been the wake-up call I'd needed.

Time to stop drifting through life filled with self-pity. Time to make a new start. Time to start living again.

"Sorry," Kye drawled, not sounding sorry in the least as he sat next to Mia, his arm draped across her shoulders as she snuggled into him. "So Dani, ready to find a hot Aussie of your own Down Under?" He smirked. "Guys in Melbourne won't know what hits them when they get a squiz at you."

"Squiz?" I wrinkled my nose. "I'm hoping that's a good thing."

He chuckled. "Means a look at you."

Mia tweaked his nose. "Isn't he adorable?"

I rolled my eyes. "You two are pathetic."

"It's luuuurv," Kye said, holding Mia tighter. "So how about it? Ready to take Melbourne by storm?"

"Academically, maybe." Because that was my number one priority. To make the most of the six months exchange program I'd been offered at the prestigious Melbourne University and start an Arts major. Thanks to Kye's dad pulling strings at the university, I had a chance at a new life. I wouldn't screw it up this time. "I can't thank your dad enough for this opportunity."

"He's the best." The visible pride in Kye's eyes made me well up again. Wish I had parents who cared enough about me to want to help my friends. "If you need anything while you're in Oz, don't hesitate to ring him."

I nodded. "That's what he told me when I Skyped him to say thanks for doing all this."

"He's a good guy." Kye's grin alerted me to another of his typical teasing barbs. "Speaking of guys—"

"Not interested." I held up my hand. "Even if you're personally acquainted with Jesse Spencer, Josh Helman and Ryan Kwanten, I don't care." I placed a hand over my heart. "I'm swearing off guys, even hot Aussie ones, for the next six months."

Mia gazed adoringly at Kye. "Never say never, sweetie." She pecked Kye on the cheek. "Trust me, there's something about Aussie guys that is irresistible."

"I'll take your word for it," I said, meaning it.

I'd spent the last three years hanging out with the wrong guys, sleeping with some of them, getting wasted, doing whatever it took to forget my fucked up life.

The next six months in Australia? My own personal detox program.

No partying, no drinking, no drugs and no men.

Mia, ever perceptive, must've picked up on something

in my expression, because she turned to Kye and said, "I'd love an orange soda."

"Coming right up." He stood and glanced at me. "Anything for you, Dani?"

I shook my head. "No thanks, I'm fine."

Biggest lie ever.

"No worries, back in a sec." He strolled toward the monstrous kitchen that included a breakfast nook complete with the latest video game consoles my dad loved. Kye would be a while. Last time he'd been here and volunteered to get us sodas, we'd found him playing some warrior shoot-out game an hour later.

The moment he left the room, Mia fixed me with a narrow-eyed stare. "You're in a funk and it's more than just living overseas for six months."

I sighed, wishing I could fob her off, but so tired of living a lie let alone telling another. "I'm terrified that even after doing all this, nothing will change and I'll still be the same screwed-up little girl screaming for attention."

Voicing my greatest fear didn't make me feel better. It made me feel sick to my stomach.

Because it was true. What if after all this I couldn't change? I couldn't forget? I couldn't learn to live with the mistakes of my past?

"Oh honey." Mia leaped off the sofa to come sit beside me on the floor. "You're the bravest person I know."

She took both my hands and wouldn't let go when I tried to extricate them. "It takes real guts to do what you're doing. Moving halfway across the world, making a start on a college degree, changing your lifestyle."

She squeezed my hands. "You've been through hell and you've made it through. This is your chance. And I have no doubt whatsoever you'll make the most of every exciting new minute."

"Will you be resurrecting your old pom-poms to go with that cheerleading routine?"

She laughed at my droll response. "You're going to be fine. Better than fine." She released my hands to pull me into a hug. "You're going to kick some serious Aussie ass."

Wish I had half her confidence because the way I was feeling now? Like I was standing on a precipice, about to go over the edge, with no safety net in sight.

ASHTON

I knew Mum was having a bad day the moment I neared her room and heard her grunts of frustration.

She'd always loved crossword puzzles but the more her brain deteriorated, the harder it became for her to do the simplest tasks, let alone find a three letter word for an Australian native bird.

I'd almost reached the end of the long corridor when a nurse laid a hand on my shoulder.

"Got a minute, Ashton?"

I stopped, turned and held my breath. Whenever one of the nurses wanted to talk before I visited Mum, it wasn't good.

"Hey Pam. How are you?"

"Good, thanks." The fifty-something redhead had the kindest eyes I'd ever seen. Pale blue eyes that were currently filled with concern. "But I wanted to have a quick word with you today."

The inevitable tension built in my temples and I quashed the urge to rub them. "Mum's okay?"

A pointless, dumb-arse question, considering Mum

hadn't been okay in a long time. Not since I'd checked her into this special accommodation home two years earlier because it had become untenable to care for her at home.

The official diagnosis? Early onset dementia courtesy of a long-term alcohol abuse problem.

My diagnosis? She'd partied too hard, done too many drugs and drunk her life into oblivion to obscure whatever demons dogged her as a washed-up B-grade actress.

I resented her lifestyle. I resented every shitty thing that resulted in her being here at the age of sixty-three.

"Judy had a rough night." Pam hesitated, before fixing me with a pitying stare. "She may not know you today."

Fuck.

We'd reached this stage already?

I'd been warned there'd be more days like this. That as the dementia progressed, Mum's memory would deteriorate to the point she'd consider me a stranger.

I hadn't expected it to happen so soon and no way in hell I was prepared to handle it.

"Okay, thanks," I said, hoping Pam didn't hear the hitch in my voice.

Not for the first time since Mum had been diagnosed, I wanted to crumple in a heap on the floor and cry like a baby. But considering I'd been the only man in this family for a long time, losing my shit wasn't an option.

I had to stand tall and do what had to be done. And that included ensuring I made enough money to pay for Mum's bills. Something that was becoming increasingly difficult to do as my commissions dried up.

I needed to keep painting. I needed to keep tutoring at the university. And I needed to stop feeling like I was an automaton, oblivious to everything but getting through each day.

It was affecting my art, this emptiness inside me. But I needed to quash emotions and stay cold inside because if I started to feel again, I'd break down for sure.

Despite her lifestyle and her failings, Mum had always done right by me. I had to do the same for her.

"You're a good son." Pam squeezed my arm. "Come find me later if you have any questions or just want to talk, okay?"

"Thanks."

I knew I wouldn't take Pam up on her offer. I could barely hold my shit together when I left here after my bi-weekly visits. No way could I face Pam's kindness, especially if Mum was as bad as expected today.

I took several deep breaths to clear the buzzing in my head and waited until I could muster a halfway normal expression, before knocking on Mum's door and entering.

"How's the crossword coming along?"

My heart twisted as her head lifted and our gazes locked. Mine deliberately upbeat. Hers eerily blank.

"Who the fuck are you?"

And with those five words, I almost lost it.

My hands shook so I stuffed them into my jacket pockets as I cautiously crossed the room to sit in an armchair opposite hers.

Keep it simple, the nurses had warned if this happened. Don't startle her or press her to remember. Be casual. As for the swearing, aggression was a common reaction in progressive dementia. But to hear the F bomb tumble from Mum's lips was as foreign to me as seeing her sitting in a pink toweling bathrobe at five in the afternoon.

She'd always been glamorous, dressed to the nines with perfect make-up from the time she rose to the time she came home from whatever party she'd attended. Even as a kid, I had memories of Mum's vivid red lipstick and strawberry-scented shampoo as she kissed me goodbye before heading to an audition, her high heels clacking on our wooden floorboards as she left me in the care of the teenager next door.

That glamorous woman was nowhere to be seen now. Her blonde hair had faded to a washed out yellowy-grey. Her brown eyes were ringed with lines and underscored by dark circles. Her shoulders were shrunken, her back curved, her muscles flaccid from lack of use.

My beautiful, exceptional mother was broken. An empty shell.

And it killed me a little bit more every time I visited.

"I'm Ashton," I said, wishing I could elaborate, wishing I could yell, 'I'm your son. The one who wiped the vomit off your face more times than I can count. Who found you passed out on the floor and carried you to bed countless times over the years. Who would do anything to have you back.'

But I said none of those things. Instead, I swallowed my resentment—at the lifestyle that had put her here—and forced a smile. "I see you're a fan of crosswords."

"Stupid bloody things." She picked up the pen she'd discarded and tapped it against the magazine. "Can you think of a five letter word for a boy's building toy?"

"Block," I said, remembering the toy sets she used to buy me when she scored a role.

I'd treasured every single one, taking my time constructing the blocks into elaborate houses or fire-stations or castles, knowing it could be a long time between jobs for Mum.

Not that she didn't try hard but she never quite cracked it for a starring role. She'd got by with TV commercials and bit parts in anything from soap operas to local feature films.

Having me at forty had changed her life.

Roles were scarce for aging actresses, especially pregnant ones. I often wondered if that had been the start of her downward spiral. If she blamed me for ruining her life.

If she did, she never showed it. Mum adored me, loving me to the point of smothering. And even as she deteriorated, partying harder to forget the fact she wasn't working much, I always came home to dinner on the table.

"Thanks." She scrawled the letters into the boxes, her hand shaky. "Could you help me do the rest?"

"Sure," I said, taking care not to startle her as I cautiously edged my chair next to hers. "I like crosswords."

Knowing I was pushing my luck, I added, "I used to do them with my Mum."

I waited, held my breath, hoping for some sign she knew who I was.

"She must be a lucky lady to have a son like you," she said, her smile wobbly as she glanced at me with those blank eyes that broke my heart.

"I'm the lucky one," I said, as I settled in to spend some time with my Mum, hoping I had the strength to do this.

Because the way I was feeling now? As brittle as tinder-dry bark, ready to snap and fly away on the slightest breeze.

I had to be stronger. Strong enough for the both of us.

READ THE REST NOW!

EXCERPT FROM BLURRING THE LINE

Annabelle's story.

Annabelle Cleary travels half way around the world...to fall in love with the boy next door all over again.

Completing her degree at a college in Denver may just be the most exciting thing this small town girl has ever done. Until she discovers her new mentor is Joel Goodes, the guy who once rocked her world.

Joel isn't a keeper. He'll break her heart again. But Annabelle can't resist the sexy Aussie at his devastating best and soon they're indulging in an all-too-brief fling.

Annabelle wants it all: career, relationship and kids, in the hometown she's always loved. The same town that holds nothing but bad memories for Joel.

When they return to Australia, will it be a homecoming they'll never forget?

ANNABELLE

Being an Aussie studying in Denver was cool. Unless your BFFs were dating hot Aussie guys and never let up on your lack of a boyfriend.

"I don't get it." Mia handed me a champers, as I thanked the gods I'd had the smarts to come to the States in my final year of uni so I could drink legally at the ripe old age of twenty-two. "You've been here a year, Annabelle, and you haven't hooked up."

Dani snorted. "Not that I blame her. Half the guys on this campus have a pole stuck so far up their asses they can hardly walk."

"Maybe she's too picky?" Mia topped up Dani's glass. "She needs to lighten up."

Dani sniggered. "And get laid."

I sipped at my champagne, content to let Mia and Dani debate my lack of male companionship. They'd been doing it the last three weeks, ever since opening night of Ashton's first art show.

Dani never shut up about Ashton, her sensitive-soul artist boyfriend. The fact she'd met him in Melbourne, while staying in my flat, kinda irked a little. During my three years doing a bachelor's degree in physiotherapy at Melbourne Uni, I'd never met a single guy I'd drool over the way Dani did with Ash.

As for Mia, she was just as pathetic with Kye, her sexy tennis jock boyfriend. With both guys being Aussie, it merely exacerbated Mia and Dani's relentless assessment of my less than stellar love life.

"How do you know I haven't hooked up or gotten laid?"

Mia clinked her glass with mine. "Because, dear friend, all you ever do is study. You don't date. You don't party."

"And you don't even consider Mia's fix-ups," Dani said, raising her glass. "Or so I've been told."

"How can I put this politely?" I finished my champers in three gulps before glaring at them. "Piss off."

Dani laughed. "I know for a fact that's the Aussie version of fuck off."

Some of the mischief faded from Mia's eyes. "You know we're only teasing?"

I nodded. "Yeah, but since the arrival of this one—" I pointed at Dani, "—you haven't let up."

Mia made a zipping motion over her lips at Dani, who was the more relentless of the two. "That's because we want you to be happy."

"I am." The quick response sounded hollow even to my ears.

Because the truth was, I wasn't happy. Sure, my studies were going great and I'd made a bunch of new friends while in Denver. But I missed Melbourne. And on a deeper level, I missed Uppity-Doo, the small country town in northern Victoria I called home.

If I was completely honest, the last time I'd been truly happy was back there, in my final year of high school, when the guy I'd adored had reciprocated my feelings on that one, fateful night I hadn't been able to forgot. Several years and a trip across the Pacific hadn't dimmed the memory. Sadly, no guy had come close to eliciting the same spark.

"Sure you are," Dani said. "You could almost convince us looking like this—" She pulled a face with downturned mouth and deep frown, "—translates to happiness in Australia." She rolled her eyes. "But I've lived there for the last twelve months, remember, and I happen to know that's bullshit."

Mia took the empty champagne glass out of my hand and draped an arm across my shoulders. "Listen, sweetie, we'll lay off if you promise to keep an open mind tonight."

"What's on tonight?" Like I had to ask. Yet another party where my well-meaning friends would try to foist some unsuspecting guy on me. A guy I'd chat with and laugh with while pretending to enjoy myself, knowing by the end of the night I'd be heading back to my dorm alone.

I wasn't interested in transient flings. Never had been. And with an expiration date on my studies here in the States, it was the main reason I'd remained single by choice.

The other reason, where I was pathetically, ridiculously hung up over a guy who didn't know I existed these days, was one I preferred to ignore.

"A few of us are heading out to that new bar in town." Mia squeezed my shoulders. "Apparently there's an Aussie guy in town Kye thought you might like to meet—"

"Not interested." I held up my hand. Yeah, like that would stop these two in full matchmaking mode. "Aussie guys are footy-loving, cricket-watching, beer-swilling bogans."

"We beg to differ." Dani smirked. "The Aussie guys we know are sexy, sweet and incredibly talented in bed."

"Hear, hear," Mia said, removing her arm from my shoulders to give Dani a high-five.

"You two are pathetic." I smiled, despite a pang of loneliness making me yearn for what they'd found with Kye and Ashton. "And for your information, I'm not going."

"That's what you think," Dani said, a second before she and Mia gang-tackled me.

We tumbled to the floor amid shrieks of laughter and hair pulling.

"Get off me." I elbowed Dani hard and followed up with a well-aimed kick to Mia's shin.

"Crazy bitch," Dani said, chuckling as she sat up and

rubbed her midriff, while Mia inspected her shin. "As if a few well-aimed jabs will get you out of going tonight."

Secretly admiring their determination to avoid me turning into a hermit, I folded my arms. "You can't make me."

"Want to make a bet?" Mia smirked. "If you don't want to come for social reasons, maybe we can appeal to your professional side."

Confused, I said, "What's that supposed to mean?"

"Apparently Kye met this guy when his shoulder tendonitis flared up today." Mia's smugness made fingers of premonition strum the back of my neck. "He's a physical therapist."

No way. It couldn't be.

"What's his name?" I aimed for casual, hoping the nerves making my stomach flip-flop wouldn't affect my voice.

Mia shrugged. "No idea."

"You'll just have to come to the bar and find out," Dani said, oblivious to the rampant adrenalin flooding my system, making me want to flee.

I was being ridiculous. There were many Australian physiotherapists working around the world. The odds of this Aussie physio being Joel were a million to one.

But that didn't stop my hands from giving a betraying quiver as I snagged my long hair that had come loose in our wrestling match and twisted it into a top-knot.

"We won't take no for an answer." Mia and Dani stood next to each other, shoulders squared, determination making their eyes glitter.

"Fine, you win." I held up my hands in resignation as they did a victory jig.

"You won't regret it, sweetie," Mia said.

I already did. Because if this Aussie physio was Joel Goodes, the guy who'd broken my heart, I was in trouble. Big trouble.

JOEL

I'd had a shit of a day.

Back to back patients for eight hours straight. Four meniscectomies, three rotator cuff tears, two carpel tunnel syndromes, an Achilles tendon bursitis, ankylosing spondylitis, torticollis, Osgood-Schlatter's, synovial cyst, popliteal effusion and a hamstring tear, and that had just been the morning.

I usually thrived on the constant buzz of diagnosing and treating orthopedic injuries at the outpatient clinic I'd worked at in downtown Denver for the last three months. The manic pace suited me.

Not today. Today, I'd been too busy mulling over Mum's late night phone call to fully appreciate the varying conditions I'd treated.

Mum was considering retiring and wanted me to come home to run her practice. A good offer, if the practice had been situated anywhere but Uppity-Doo.

God, I hated that name. Hated what it stood for more. Staidness. Stability. Stifling. Small town fishbowl mentality with a healthy dose of outback narrow-mindedness. Not that Uppity-Doo was outback exactly. Situated close to the Victorian-New South Wales border, it was four hours from Melbourne. And a million miles from where I ever wanted to be.

I'd escaped the town as soon as I could. Did my physio bachelor's degree in Melbourne and had been travelling ever since. Four years on the road. Locum work from

London to LA, and many cities in between. Three months in one city was ideal, six months at a stretch.

I'd been enjoying my stint in Denver, until that phone call. Mum's bollocking, about how I'd skirted responsibility all these years, rankled. She needed someone to take over her practice. That someone couldn't be me.

So when my last patient of the day, an Aussie tennis player, had invited me to a bar with some of his mates tonight, I'd accepted. A few beers would take the edge off.

But it wouldn't eradicate the inevitable guilt that talking to Mum elicited. She sure knew how to ram the bamboo under my fingernails and hammer the buggers home. She'd been the same with Dad. And it had killed him in the end.

I entered the bar and made for the pool tables, where Kye Sheldon had said his group would be. Would be good to chat to a bunch of fellow Aussies. Not that I didn't appreciate the people I met on my travels, but nobody did laid-back humor like Aussies.

"Mate, good to see you." Kye appeared out of nowhere as I neared the tables and slapped me on the back. "Come meet the rest of the gang."

A boutique beer was thrust at me by a guy on my left. "Cheers, mate. I'm Ashton."

"Thanks." I raised the bottle in his direction. "Been in the States long?"

"About a month." Ashton pointed at Kye. "This bloke's practically a local though."

Kye grinned. "Can't tear myself away from the joint."

Ashton snorted. "That's because his girlfriend has his balls in her back pocket."

I laughed and Kye held up his hands in surrender. "Guilty as charged, and loving it."

These guys had an obvious camaraderie and I experienced a rare pang. Traveling continuously wasn't conducive to mateship and I missed having someone, anyone, I could rely on.

I'd had a good mate once, back in Uppity-Do. A mate I'd eventually lost contact with deliberately, because of what I'd done with his sister.

Man, Trevor would've killed me if he'd found out about Annabelle and me.

"You can talk." Kye pressed his thumb into Ashton's forehead. "Yep, my thumb fits perfectly into the permanent indentation Dani has left there."

Ashton clinked his beer bottle against Kye's. "I'm a schmuck in love and proud of it."

They turned to face me. "What about you, Joel? You seeing anyone?"

I shook my head. "I move around too much to maintain a relationship."

The flash of pity in their eyes surprised me. Usually guys in relationships envied my lifestyle. And freedom was enviable. Not being tied down to one woman, in one place, for all eternity. Dying a slow death.

Ashton nodded, thoughtful. "Relationships are hard work, without the added pressure of distance."

"Listen to you." Kye sniggered. "Next you'll be braiding our hair and painting our nails."

Ashton's eyes narrowed but he grinned. "Dani likes that I'm a SNAG."

"You're not a sensitive new age guy, you're a lapdog." Kye lowered his tone and leaned toward me. "He's an *artist*. That explains a lot."

In response, Ashton punched Kye on the arm. Considering the size of the tennis player's biceps I'd seen while treating his shoulder earlier today, he wouldn't feel a thing.

"Better than being a Neanderthal masquerading as a college student while playing tennis for fun." Ashton made inverted comma signs with his fingers when he said 'for fun' and smirked.

I chuckled. "You two are like an old married couple. Been mates for long?"

"A month," Kye said, which surprised me. Ashton had said he'd been in the States a month but from their obvious bond I'd assumed they'd known each other longer. "Our girlfriends are besties, so since Ashton came over with Dani for his first art show, we've been hanging around a lot."

Ashton raised his beer in Kye's direction. "But lucky for me, I'll be heading back to Melbourne in a few weeks, leaving this funny man behind."

"You'll miss me," Kye said, deadpan.

"Like a hole in the head," Ashton muttered, his amused gaze drawn to the door behind me. "Don't look now, Sheldon, but your balls just made an appearance."

Kye elbowed Ashton and the artist winced a little.

"'About time the girls showed up," Kye said, waving. "Don't worry, mate, they've brought a friend so you won't feel like a third wheel."

Shit, this better not be some lame fix-up. I wanted to have a few beers to unwind, not feel compelled to make mindless small talk with some chick I wouldn't see after tonight.

"She's a real hottie, too," Ashton said, elbowing me. "Check her out."

I glanced over my shoulder, the epitome of casual, and froze.

Because I knew the petite redhead with the killer bod striding toward me. Knew her intimately. And damned if my cock didn't harden at the memory.

Annabelle Cleary. The only good thing to come out of Uppity-Doo. And one of the reasons I'd bolted as fast as I goddamned could from that shithole town.

Kye bumped me. "What do you think?"

I am so screwed.

READ THE REST NOW!

EXCERPT FROM BEFORE

If you enjoyed this book, check out my other New Adult contemporary romance **BEFORE**, available **FREE** at all retailers.

Good girls finish last? Screw that.

Being a small town girl isn't so bad. Unless Mom's the town joke and I've spent my entire life shying away from her flamboyance. College in Las Vegas should be so much cooler. But it's not. Bad things happen. Real bad.

So when my brother Reid offers me an all-expenses paid vacation to Australia for a month, I am so there. Discounting the deadly snakes on the outback cattle station, I should be safe.

Until I meet Jack.

Jack defines bad boy and then some. He's big, buffed, bronzed, and hotter than any guy I've ever met. His sexy Aussie accent makes me melt. And the guy can cook.

But he's my brother's new bestie and he lives on the other side of the world. There's no future for us.

Is there?

JESS

College was overrated. Seriously.

The dorm-hopping, frat-partying, alcohol-imbibing rumors were true. The part where I became a party animal, made a zillion BFFs and took UNLV by storm? Hadn't kicked in yet. I sucked as badly as a freshman at the University of Nevada, Las Vegas, as I had as a student at Hell High, my nickname for my old high school in Craye Canyon. Apparently once a geek, always a geek.

In two semesters I'd attended three frat parties, had drunk two vodkas, one rum and a watered down Long Island Iced Tea. And the only other bed I'd graced besides my own belonged to my roommate's dog, illegally smuggled in whenever she could. Yeah, chalk up permanent virginity status alongside geek. Embarrassing.

On the upside, I didn't live at home any more. One of the major incentives for busting my ass at high school to enroll at UNLV was the distance. UNVL was over an hour away from my hometown so I'd have to live on campus. Craye Canyon wasn't big enough for Mom and me.

Pity my foray into freedom hadn't lived up to expectations. I'd hoped to shed my good-girl image at college. Yet here I was, last day before summer break, still hanging out in the library. Worse? Still a virgin.

"Hey Jess, you're coming tonight, yeah?"

I glanced across at Dave, my study partner, and bit back my first response of 'I wish.' Somehow, I didn't think the serious bookworm would appreciate the innuendo.

"Think I'll give it a miss," I said, packing my satchel for the last time this semester.

I was free for the summer. Without plans. I couldn't head home, not with Mom in wedding planner frenzy mode. Summer was the busiest month for Nevada weddings and it seemed like every bridezilla in the state wanted Pam Harper to organize their wedding. Poor suckers.

"School's out, Geekette." Dave tweaked my nose. "Time to par-tay."

"That settles it." I elbowed him away. "No way am I going anywhere with a dork who says *par-tay*."

"Now you're just playing hard to get." Dave slung an arm across my shoulder, a friendly gesture I'd tolerated during our many study sessions together.

"Yeah, that's me, a regular babe juggling guys along with assignments." I rolled my eyes. "Besides, I've got plans tonight."

"What plans?" He snapped his fingers. "Quick, the truth, before you make up some crap."

"I haven't seen my cousin in a while, thought I'd hang out with her."

Truth was, my cousin Chantal worked nights as a dancer at the coolest burlesque venue on the Strip. But she had a great apartment I could hide out in to avoid the inevitable end of semester parties.

I didn't feel like getting drunk, stoned or laid. Not that I'd ever done any of those things before. That Geekette nickname Dave had bestowed on me last August when we both started our undergrad English major? Pathetically true.

"Come to the party with me for a while, then go hang with your cousin later."

When I opened my mouth to protest again, Dave pressed his finger against my lips. "Not talking no for an answer, got it?"

I didn't mind Dave's arm around my shoulder but having his finger against my mouth made me uncomfortable. We were friends. We hung out. Two loners who studied and grabbed the occasional meal. I wasn't remotely attracted to the six foot, reed-thin Mr. Average and I'd never picked up any vibes off him.

But there was something about the way he was looking at me, the way he was muscling in on my personal space, that had me edging away.

"I might see you there," I said, slinging my bag over my shoulder and accidentally on purpose bumping him out of the way in the process.

For a second I thought I glimpsed anger in his pale grey eyes before he blinked and I attributed it to the sunlight filtering through the library windows.

"Okay, catch you later."

I waited until Dave left, watching him lope between the tables and out the main library doors. I liked his easy-going nature, how he joked around without crossing the line. He'd never put the moves on me so the whole touchy-feely finger on the lips? Probably harmless and just me over-reacting to having a long, hot summer stretching ahead of me with not one freaking thing to do.

I needed to get a life.

Fast.

JACK

I was a man on a mission.

I needed a bourbon in one hand and a blonde in the other, not necessarily in that order. And the annual Onakie B&S Ball happily provided both.

I'd traveled a long, dusty three hundred miles to attend

the black tie Bachelor and Spinster ball in outback Queensland, along with ten thousand other revelers currently jammed into the arena.

Festivities—translated: consuming as much alcohol as humanly possible—had kicked off in the afternoon, gates to the ball opened at seven, which meant there were a lot of B&S's paired off already. Nothing like beer goggles for making a member of the opposite sex appear overly attractive.

I hadn't run into anyone I knew, which suited me just fine. No one from the Cooweer Homestead cattle station where I worked had made the long trek. Then again, considering I was the only twenty-year-old on the property, with the next youngest employee being forty-five, it didn't surprise me. Besides, I preferred it this way. A few hours out of my mundane life to cut free. Go wild. Get pissed. Shag some willing and able chick.

It may not be much, but after spending the last four months working my arse off at the cattle station as a cook, I needed to burn off a little steam.

"Hey handsome. Gotta light?" A thirty-something blonde with sun-wrinkles ringing her big blue eyes touched my forearm, waving a cigarette in her other hand at me.

I shook my head. "Sorry. Don't smoke."

"Too bad." She flung the cigarette away and stepped in closer. "Fancy a drink instead?"

"Got one, thanks." I raised my bourbon. "But don't let me stop you."

Not deterred by my offhand responses, she threaded her fingers through mine. "Let's go dance." She paused and sent me a loaded glance from beneath her lash extensions. "Down by the river."

Code for 'my Ute is parked at the farthest corner of the

compound so we can fuck our brains out and no one will hear.'

This is exactly what I'd wanted. A no-strings-attached quickie to alleviate the boredom. So why did the thought of having meaningless sex with a stranger suddenly sound so unappealing?

She stood on her tiptoes and whispered in my ear. "I give great head."

I wasn't too keen, but my cock wasn't so discerning. It stood to attention, straining to get at the brazen blonde.

Sensing my indecision, she tugged on my hand. "Come on."

Like any weak-minded guy who allowed the wrong head to dictate his actions, I fell into step beside her. We dodged a crammed dance floor where an international rock band blasted hard core. We pushed our way through wall-to-wall revelers drunk on booze and each other. We wound our way through Utes and 4WDs parked helter-skelter. We sidestepped couples writhing against each other in the dark.

It was nothing I hadn't seen before. In fact, in the four years since I'd run from the last foster home in Sydney and worked my away across the outback to far north Queensland, I'd attended several B&S balls like this. Lonely people from all walks of life hooking up for a night of raucous fun, endless drinking and faceless sex.

I was over it.

"Here we are." She paused at the last Ute in a haphazard row. I couldn't see its color in the dark but it had an impressive chrome bull bar that shimmered in the moonlight. "You up for it?"

Before I could respond, she had her hand on my cock and her mouth on mine.

I wanted sex. Looked like I was about to get it.

Her tongue dueled with mine, demanding and taunting, as she unzipped me.

I groaned when her hand wrapped around my cock and pulled me free. She squeezed and pulled, teasing me, before dropping to her knees.

The moment her mouth closed around my cock, I closed my eyes, savoring the suction. Just the right amount. No teeth. A skillful gliding action of her mouth that milked me in wet velvet.

She was right. She gave frigging great head.

My balls tightened in anticipation but she was good at this, because she knew the right moment to stop sucking, fish a foil packet out of her bra and roll a condom on me in the time it took for my lust-hazed brain to clear.

"Very nice." She licked her lips with a slow, deliberate sweep of her tongue, before pushing me backward so I was lying flat on my back on the tray of her Ute. "Bet you feel as good as you taste."

She hoisted up her black satin gown and straddled me, giving me a nice eyeful of Brazilian, which she proceeded to play with. Her finger circled her clit as she sank down on me with a moan that raised the hairs on my arms.

There was something incredibly sexy about an uninhibited older woman bouncing up and down on the end of my cock, so into it that I was nothing but an adjunct to her pleasure.

It didn't take long for either of us. She brought herself to orgasm as she slammed down on me at a frantic pace, impaling herself so hard I saw stars when I came. Though that could've literally been the stars clustered in the clear outback sky framed behind her.

"How old are you?" she said as she clambered off and

headed around the side of the Ute to the cabin, giving me time to take care of the condom and zip up.

"Twenty."

She glanced up from the side mirror where she was busy reapplying a vivid red lip-gloss. "That's great. I've always wanted to fuck a guy half my age."

She beamed like I'd just presented her with the best gift ever, while my gut twisted. Guess I was as good at judging women's ages as I was at making decisions about where my life was headed. Absolutely shithouse.

Was this really what I wanted? Working my arse off cooking for a bunch of non-appreciative pricks for months on end, then spending my down time screwing old chicks?

My life was officially down the crapper.

"Thanks," she said, patting my cheek. "I'm heading back to the ball. See you round."

Not if I could help it and it wasn't until she disappeared from view that I realized we hadn't even exchanged names.

Fuck.

There had to be more to life than this.

READ THE REST FOR FREE!

ABOUT THE AUTHOR

USA TODAY bestselling and multi-award winning author Nicola Marsh writes page-turning fiction to keep you up all night.
She's published 82 books and writes contemporary romance, domestic suspense, and fantasy.
She's also a Waldenbooks, Bookscan, Amazon, iBooks, and Barnes & Noble bestseller, a RBY (Romantic Book of the Year) and National Readers' Choice Award winner, and a multi-finalist for numerous other awards, including the RITA.
A physiotherapist for thirteen years, she now adores writing full time, raising her two dashing young heroes, barracking loudly for her Kangaroos football team, sharing fine food with family and friends, and her favorite, curling up with a good book!